# MEN OF
# THE MANOR

# MEN OF THE MANOR

## EROTIC ENCOUNTERS BETWEEN UPSTAIRS LORDS & DOWNSTAIRS LADS

EDITED BY
ROB ROSEN

**CLEiS**
PRESS

Published in the United States by Cleis Press Inc., 2246 Sixth Street, Berkeley, California 94710.

Printed in the United States.
Cover design: Scott Idleman/Blink
Cover photograph: Copyright © 2014 by Louis LaSalle, louislasalle.com
Text design: Frank Wiedemann
First Edition.
10 9 8 7 6 5 4 3 2 1

Trade paper ISBN: 978-1-62778-066-7
E-book ISBN: 978-1-62778-078-0

For Kenny,
forever the lord of my manor

# Contents

ix   *Introduction*

1   *The Maze* • DALE CHASE

16   *Finnias Laredo* • ALEX STITT

35   *Finsloe* • XAVIER AXELSON

54   *Booting* • SALOME WILDE

68   *Seducing the Footman* • BRENT ARCHER

81   *Folly's Ditch* • FELICE PICANO

97   *Manor Games* • MICHAEL ROBERTS

110   *Brass Rags* • J. L. MERROW

132   *Mutable Memories* • MICHAEL BRACKEN

145   *Front Door, Back Door* • LOGAN ZACHARY

166   *Chauffeur's Hole* • LANDON DIXON

178   *Master Jeffy Learns a Lesson* • SASHA PAYNE

202   *Bohemian Rhapsody* • ROB ROSEN

215   *About the Authors*

218   *About the Editor*

# INTRODUCTION

The estates are huge and sprawling, and the fashionably elite have too much time on their hands, while the toiling underclass are always on the lookout for a means to a brighter tomorrow. Thus begins *Men of the Manor,* whose stories—whether it's the wildly funny Michael Roberts's "Manor Games," or the spicy tale of blackmail in Landon Dixon's "Chauffeur's Hole," or the opening saga, "The Maze," by Dale Chase, with its land-owner who's desperate to keep his fortunes—all contain twists and turns and enough sex to make the town vicar blush. Still, *Men of the Manor,* at its core, is about handsome lords and upper-class gents, humpy footmen and scheming valets. Throw in period costumes, sumptuous settings, unbridled passion, tortured characters with deep, dark secrets, villainous masters and heroic servants, not to mention a scandal or two, and what you end up with is an incredible collection filled to the page-turning brim with class warfare and high drama, where the great equalizer is the promise of a tumble on the canopied bed, all of it joyously brought to you by some of today's best and brightest erotica writers, such as Salome Wilde, Logan Zachary, and famed author Felice Picano, just to name a few. So sit back, relax and turn off that PBS and BBC, because I am about to bring you a saucy assortment that makes their offerings pale in comparison.

Rob Rosen
San Francisco

# THE MAZE

## Dale Chase

Aconsoling wife was the last thing I wanted.

"Do as you must, Preston," she said. "We've survived other difficulties and we shall survive this."

I hadn't wanted agreement. Quite the opposite, I wanted argument. I wanted a plea not to sell Hambly Hall before it bankrupted me. Generations had managed to keep it going, and the last thing I wanted was to be the one who failed. I counted on Sylvia to make the stand I could not.

"I'll give it more thought," I said, turning from her and walking out onto the terrace. She was kind not to follow.

Gazing upon the vast lawns and gardens, I saw both paradise and hell: the paradise of childhood consumed by the searing reality that modern times could not provide the resources needed to maintain such an estate. Stepping from the terrace to a path below, I attempted to leave such concerns behind, but they clung to me like sticky paper on my shoe.

Two possibilities loomed: sell part of the land and attempt

to maintain the balance of the estate on the proceeds or sell the whole damned thing while I could still hold my head high, then take up residence in some seaside cottage and disappear into commonality. The boy in me wanted to hold on while the man was forced to face a cruel reality: it was time to let the place go.

I hurried my step, as if I could outrun the awful truth, and when I reached the upper garden, I fixed upon its burst of color and accompanying sweet scent, finding, as always, that they soothed both man and boy. Bees buzzed among the blooms while birds chirped approval from nearby trees. I savored the sunshine while behind me the house loomed like some black shroud.

Hambly Hall's manor house was an imposing three-story structure of forty-two rooms. Surrounding it were sculpted gardens, lawns, orchards and, on the eastern side, a maze. I walked there now for no reason but that of the boy seeking solitude. The maze had been a childhood refuge when things in the house upset me or, as I matured, when I sought the privacy a young man requires to address certain physical aspects. At five I'd imagined the place a magical castle filled with knights to protect me. At ten it was a forest where lived a friendly unicorn. At fifteen it was the private place where I explored the sexuality that had burst upon me and become so rampant that I could scarcely contain it.

I knew every inch of the maze and could reach the center without calling up the mental map I'd made as a child. Now, as I reached the sacred place, I couldn't recall my last visit. So many years had passed without my seeking refuge among the tall and crisply maintained hedges that I felt a certain loss, and so, as I entered, I looked to embrace the comfort once known amid its confines.

Gardeners kept the estate grounds in fine shape, spending

much time trimming the maze to crisp edges. It didn't matter how little it was used; I insisted it be kept up at all times, and so a man was usually working there, the steady clip of shears always welcome.

I paused at the entrance and looked back at Hambly Hall, where I wondered if Sylvia watched my progress. Dear woman, she truly had no concept of the things that drive a man, the depth of the responsibilities that hound him, and the need for respite. She had only to plan meals and order servants about, leaving her husband to shoulder all else. At times I envied her.

Entering the maze, I automatically turned left and at the first juncture went right. These steps warmed me, and I felt much the child having no greater concern than finding a unicorn. On I went, turning this way and that without having to pause and decide which path to take. The route was imprinted on me and, if circumstances forced me to leave Hambly Hall, I'd take that imprint with me.

As I went along, I ran a hand against the hedges, eight-foot-high privets thick with age. Their core was woody and hard while the outer layer was soft and green, giving off a familiar scent I inhaled to excess. Turning and turning again, I moved along steadily but without hurry, knowing I'd soon reach the heart where sat the iron bench on which I'd indulged in unicorns and other things.

I encountered no gardener this morning, but the hedges looked trim, so the men were likely working elsewhere. Then, as I made the next-to-last turn, I heard sounds of a man in distress—or so I first thought. Grunts came through the privet, as if someone was being tugged on or perhaps a man had fallen from a ladder, was injured and unable to summon help. I hurried around the next turn to the center, but stopped at the entrance when I saw there was in fact no distress.

Stepping back so I wouldn't be seen, I kept close enough to have a good view because I was stunned far more than had been the boy by his unicorn. Standing behind the bench and clutching its back was Knox, the young gardener's assistant hired mere weeks before. His trousers were down and he was bent to allow Doyle, the head gardener, to fuck him. Doyle, a big and rough man I seldom spoke to, had his trousers open to allow his cock up the boy, and it was from him that the grunting issued in time to each thrust into the young bottom. Shocked at the sight, my first thought was retreat, but this quickly gave way to my own cock stirring. I made no move to turn from the spectacle. Instead, I put a hand to my crotch, as I was coming up hard.

I knew of such activity between men, but had never witnessed it, nor considered it might take place on these grounds. Unlawful and certainly immoral, I thought that it should be stopped here and now and that it was I who should intervene. But I made no such move. As the fuck continued, I undid my trousers and put a hand inside.

I held my swollen member as Doyle allowed his prick to escape the boy and then ride back up between his buttocks like a great fleshy sword. He thrust as such for several strokes, and I noted how big the cock was, flushed bright pink and wet with his juices. Then it went back up the boy who had now gotten a hand on his own prick and was going at himself with a fury. At this I pulled my cock free of its confines and began working myself, my entire being caught up in a depravity so overwhelming I could not help but indulge.

I'd brought myself off many a time as a grown man, so that was nothing new. Sylvia often wouldn't have me, and I'd retreat to my dressing room where I'd gain relief by my own hand. She knew I did this, and though she never spoke on it, being a lady,

I'm sure she approved, as it spared her what she thought a messy and intrusive practice.

Pumping away, Doyle's grunts became louder until at last he growled like a bear. His face reddened and, as he took on the grimace common to all men when they come, I let go my own spurts, a climax of great proportion sweeping over me. As Doyle and I simultaneously emptied, the boy gave a cry, his *stuff* spewing onto the bench.

Spent, I attempted to regain my breath while slumping from the joyous release. In this state, I did not immediately notice that Doyle had withdrawn from the boy and was looking at me. I had, in my throes, it seemed, moved out where I could be seen.

My cock had softened upon its completion, but I still held on, unwilling to let the moment pass. Doyle let go of Knox, and while the boy scampered to pull up his pants, Doyle made no move for cover, and neither did I.

Once buttoned up, the boy ran past me, and I said not a word while Doyle took a few steps my way. His prick had lost its stiffness, but still possessed some girth and appeared naturally large. As I kept my gaze fixed upon it, Doyle took it in hand. "It's a big 'un," he said, and I looked up. He was coarse, as are most outdoor men, well over six feet and thick of build. Plain featured, brown haired, and ruddy from the sun, he nevertheless gave off an appeal that kept me stirred, no matter I'd just come.

"You want me to fuck you?" he asked with a leer. "I can get it up again, as I'm a virile sort, having more spunk in my balls than do most stallions." He took a couple of steps my way, and I drew back, as if distance could quell the flame he'd ignited. "Ever had a cock up you?" he then asked. "I'm thinking not. You've got milady, and while a cunt ain't a bad place to stick your cock, true satisfaction is gained only by taking one up the arse." Here he wagged his thing. I noticed it was quickly regaining size. "That's right," Doyle continued. "I can get it up right now, so drop your trousers and I'll break you in. Nobody need know. Just you and me." The leer rose on his face.

My mouth went dry and my heart raced as I fought the urge to engage in depravity. I wanted to take hold of that big prick, fondle and play with the thing, maybe suck on it. I hadn't touched any cock but my own since school, where all young boys experimented. Now, here before me was a man's own specimen, large and eager. I could almost feel it in my palm.

"Well, come on then," prodded Doyle, stepping closer.

It struck me then that he meant to put it up me, and I caught myself, for the lord of the manor showing his prick to a servant, or worse, the servant thinking he might take advantage, would never do. Appalled at this turn, I stuffed my cock into my trousers, buttoned up and fled, but by the time I reached the house I'd shed the panic in favor of recalling Doyle's massive prick.

I sought my study, as I could not possibly face Sylvia in such a state. I sat at my desk and attempted to review accounts while knowing it futile. At last, I gave way and turned to look out the window, grateful the view was not that of the maze. This didn't matter, of course; the incident was seared into memory, driving off all lesser images. After some minutes of turmoil, I decided there was no need to resist what was so thoroughly upon me. I brought to mind Doyle fucking the boy, the image of which sprang up like he was going at it there in my study. I'd never seen men fuck, and found it intoxicating, a cock up a man's bottom instead of a woman's well-guarded cunt. Men would have no such guard, welcoming all that was offered, the need constant. It was a wonderfully filthy idea, and it instantly began to rouse me.

When I sought my dressing room and found my valet there

attending my suits, I felt much the boy caught with prick in hand. "You may go, Hodge," I rasped. He passed me a questioning look, though I'm certain I gave not a hint that my cock was stiffening.

"Very good, sir," he said as he retreated.

Once alone, I stripped naked, need upon me as never before. This surprised me, as a climax with Sylvia always brought on sleep; this time it fueled me anew, and so, once bare, I stood at the mirror and handled my prick while revisiting the scene in the maze. As I saw Doyle's heavy prick going up the boy's bottom, a craving came over me so powerfully that it had to be addressed. I turned my backside to the mirror and with my free hand put a finger up my exposed hole.

There came no disgust at this. Rather, a wave of pleasure washed through my passage, my cock thickening in my hand. I then began to prod myself while pulling my rod and knew near ecstasy until I realized the penetration inadequate. What I wanted was something cock-like. Popping out the finger, I looked around for some long implement with which to spear myself and found it in a walking stick. Old and seldom used, it was unadorned and bore no rubber tip; it was simply rounded on the end. Imagining it a wooden prick, I grabbed hold of it, squatted at the mirror, and eased it up myself while watching it go in. A cry of pleasure attempted to escape me, and I had to work at remaining silent.

It quickly became obvious that I needed lubrication for this effort, so I left my dressing room, crossed the bedroom, and entered Sylvia's dressing room, after knocking to make sure she was absent. Alone among her pots and jars, I took up a large gob of cream and hurried back to my sex grotto. I smeared the stuff on the stick and ran some up my hole, then squatted and inserted the stick once again, imagining it was

the cock of an aroused man who was urgent in his need to
have me. I then proceeded to fuck myself while pulling my
rod to a massive come, and it was then that I got what Doyle
meant about having something up the backside. As I fucked
and came, I watched it all in the mirror, which only increased
the pleasure.

Once spent, however, shame fell upon me, and the sight of
the stick in me became revolting. I withdrew it, wiped it with a
towel, and put it away, then cleaned my spunk from the floor,
lest Hodge find it. Once the evidence was gone, I was left to
face myself in the mirror, and what I'd done did not sit well
with me, the lord of the manor having fucked himself. It was
appalling, and I immediately dressed and went down to Sylvia,
who I found reading in the front parlor. "Dearest," I said when
I reached her. I kissed her cheek, then took up a newspaper and
settled in a chair opposite, life now as it should be.

I understandably avoided the maze from then on out, though
one time I did glance that way. Sight of a ladder set up against
it aroused me to such extent that I approached Sylvia in bed
that night. She was good at her wifely duty, allowing her gown
removed, but once I was fully possessed of a throbbing erection,
I asked her if we might progress in our lovemaking.

"Of course, dearest," she cooed. "In what way?"

"I want you to put a finger up me while I'm aroused."

She stiffened in my embrace. "*Up* you?"

"My bottom hole. It's a highly sensitive area for a man. Just
put it in and work it around, maybe in and out as well."

She pulled away. "That is disgusting," she declared, and
before I could say anything more, she pulled on her gown and
fled to her dressing room. I lay there expecting the familiar
shame a man inflicts on himself when he makes reasonable

demands on his wife that are seen by her as unreasonable, but this time there came no such shame. What I found was a relief of sorts, so I fled to my dressing room, sought my stick, applied cream that I'd now stocked, and proceeded to fuck myself to a most satisfying come. I decided then that I need not trouble Sylvia with further demands.

The next day, when I again saw a ladder at the maze, I ventured there. I wanted to see Doyle's cock again, but not as he went at a boy who couldn't possibly appreciate what he received. Making the usual turns in the maze, I feared Doyle might be absent, the ladder simply not yet put away. My prick, however, thought otherwise, and by the time I reached the center bench, I was fully erect. Much to my disappointment, I found myself alone.

I paced the little garden square that was no bigger than a parlor, my arousal unrelenting. Finally I sat, undid my pants, and got out my cock. Eyes closed, I sat working it until I heard a voice. "Come to call, did you?" said Doyle.

I opened my eyes to see him in front of me.

"Brought me something, I see," he added, nodding at my prick. He began to undo his trousers, and once open he pushed them down so I might enjoy not only his formidable cock, but the black thicket from which it sprang.

My gaze fixed upon the sight as I continued to work myself. In response, Doyle began to pull his rod with one hand while the other fondled his balls. "You'll have to get them trousers down if you want it," he said as he moved closer.

The cock was so much fatter than the walking stick that it scared as well as excited me. As if to read my thoughts, Doyle said, "Don't worry. It'll fit up you. The arsehole stretches for a fuck as it welcomes such a thing. A man's true center is up there, and once it's attended by a cock, it sets up a craving you cannot deny. Now, get your pants and drawers down, as I'm in need of a fine old fuck."

He continued pulling his cock, and I found myself on my feet, removing first my coat, as it might impede things, then undoing my trousers. When I pushed them down along with my linen, Doyle grabbed me and pulled me to my feet. "Lean against the back of the bench and stick out your bum," he commanded.

I looked around, which was silly as we were truly alone, then hobbled around the back of the bench and took hold while thrusting my bottom at him like some bitch in heat. When he parted my buttocks, I issued a little cry.

"Okay then," he said, and I felt his wet knob poke at my puckered hole. Even this thrilled me, the awful place now part of sex play. He nudged and pushed, then gave a good shove and popped it in, at which I cried out, pain shooting through me. "Won't hurt for long," he said as he began to fuck. "Pleasure will take you over, I guarantee."

He was right. Amid the pain, I found a feeling beyond any previously known, the cock now well inside me and addressing places most sensitive. I grabbed my prick, as I wanted to come with him fucking me.

"Good, ain't it?" he said.

I nodded a reply. He laughed, never breaking stride.

"You've a tight passage, milord," he declared. "Makes for a fine fuck. Yes sir, fine indeed."

I was beyond ecstasy, and when a climax beckoned, I began to utter the gibberish of a man lost to his most intimate function. I could not remain still, either in body or voice. I squealed and moaned as his cock went in and out, sending my passage into a throb that saw my prick ready to fire.

"Fuck the stuff outa ya," growled Doyle.

In return, I managed the only words that mattered. "Fuck me, fuck me."

In response, he rammed harder, and as his spurts began, I pumped out my own, which went on and on, likely due to the rear activity. Never had I gained such powerful release. He, meanwhile, went a good distance, going at me for an impressive period, but at last we were spent and he pulled out. I hated to relinquish him, as I now knew the joys of rear occupation. I was now broken in, and I already wanted more.

When he withdrew, I turned to view the big cock, which was red, wet and still half-hard. "Gave you a good load," he said as his weapon took the air. "You let go too."

"Yes, quite," I replied, not wanting to speak at such a moment.

"You let me suck you, and I can get it up for another go," he informed me. As I heard this boast, I felt his spunk run down my leg, decadence stirring me anew. I'd not let go of my cock but released it now, as if to allow him upon me further when I had no such intention. Or so I thought.

Doyle wasted no time. Before I could utter a word, he dropped to his knees and sucked my soft cock into his mouth. He then began to feast on me while pulling his prick.

I had never before been sucked. Sylvia refused such activity, calling it a disgusting practice and berating me for even its very mention. Women I'd known sexually before my marriage had said much the same, yet here was a man willing not only to take me into his mouth but to do wondrous things therein.

I looked down as he licked and sucked, thrilled at him attending me thusly. I didn't come up hard, due to such a large spend just before, but no matter. I liked my prick being worked by a knowledgeable tongue that at times seemed to wrap around it. When he fell to sucking my knob, I nearly swooned. He kept at me until his cock was stiff, at which time he finally let me go. His eyes were wild now, as if he'd not yet taken satisfaction.

"Strip off below," he said.

"Beg pardon?"

He laughed. "Naked below. No trousers or drawers." When I stood idle, he commanded, "Do it!"

I undressed entirely below the waist, nakedness adding to my excitement.

"On the ground, on your back," said Doyle.

"No," I replied, as this was unthinkable.

Again the laugh. "You married ones never want it frontways, thinking it wifely, but once I'm in you, you'll forget all that. I like to look at the face of the man I fuck, so lie back and raise your legs."

I sank to the ground, and when I didn't put up my legs, he did it, placing them on his shoulders as he scooted into position. Sylvia came to mind, though I'd never put her legs so high; knees up was all I got. Still, him at me this way was awful. Wonderfully awful.

When he entered me, I grabbed my cock, because he went in deeper this time. "What'd I tell ya?" he said with a chuckle. "Now let's have us a fucking good fuck."

Having come before, he was not quick, and I did not mind in the least. I also found I liked being taken in this position as it seemed more welcoming on my part and I wanted him to know this was very much the case. Raising the legs to admit a man told that man something, allowed him use of me, allowed my vulnerability. All this I considered as the cock thrust in and out, Doyle's gaze steady upon me. When I took hold of my prick again, he nodded encouragement. "Give it a pull," he said, and I began to work it, not counting on a response.

The sun was overhead when we began, and after awhile I

noted its movement. This led me to consider Doyle a man of great prowess, every bit as virile as he'd boasted. He kept at me, my passage lubricated by his earlier issue, which had now liquefied. I felt sloppy inside, and the pain I'd first known had vanished. I'd stretched to accommodate the big cock. "Fuck me," I pled, my eyes fixed on his. "Fuck me."

He rammed his reply into me while I squealed. "You want more?" he asked. Before I could respond, he pushed my legs up around my ears, which allowed him to bore down into me, getting the big prick well up into my bowels, until I thought I might faint.

At last, when he was dripping with sweat and smelling more horse than man, he began to growl. His thrusts became urgent and his expression screwed up into the unmistakable one of climax. Then he roared and came. I felt a flush up into me, and I clenched my muscle to receive his issue. He pumped a bit more, then pulled out, his breath labored, face red. I looked at the big cock, surprisingly still substantial. "It'll quiet down now," Doyle panted, taking it in hand and giving it a pull that I saw as the equivalent of patting a horse after a good run.

"Hard to believe it's ever quiet," I replied.

He let go of my legs, and I brought them down on either side of him. Expecting him to jump up, I was surprised he didn't rush away. He looked me in the eye like he wished to couple there as well, and I held his gaze out of respect for his accomplishments. Then he gave out a laugh and got up. I sought my clothes and stood to dress.

"I'll walk out ahead," I said, when we had righted ourselves. "You wait a few minutes before leaving."

He said nothing, and I saw we were back to master and servant, which likely brought him discomfort in light of what he'd just done. "I'll visit you again," I told him. "Put the ladder up at the entrance to tell me you're within."

He passed me a hard look that I took to mean that he saw himself now entitled to further congress. Wishing to assure him, I said, "I will be back." He nodded, and I left him there.

Walking to the house, I was most pleasantly conscious of what Doyle had deposited in my passage. He'd fucked me, I thought. As if to confirm this, more of his spunk ran from my bottom. My linen would be soaked. What surprised me was finding this welcome rather than objectionable. I decided to not relinquish it to the laundry but to keep it in my dressing room, evidence of our coupling, his actual issue which I prized doubly so for having run out of me. My steps slowed as I savored not only the promise of decadent private moments, but further visits to the maze. Though I knew Doyle had buttoned up and gone back to work, I thought of him still exposed, cock stiff in recall of our congress.

Partway to the manor house, I slowed to look upon its grandeur once more, a grandeur I had thought to relinquish. How could I have considered such action? It seemed truly impossible to allow anyone but me to inhabit this magnificent hall. I would work toward resurrecting its profitability, work toward restoring the majesty that was its due. There was no need for retreat. I was lord of the manor and fully capable of great things. Stopping to take it all in with a grand sweep of the eye, I saw the black shroud now fallen away, saw the ancient stone and heavy columns, saw ivy-draped walls and flowers bursting forth at the base. Hambly Hall would not only remain in my hands, it would thrive.

When I encountered Sylvia on the terrace, she smiled. "I see you've been in the maze," she made note, taking my arm.

"I have," I replied, savoring the wetness in my drawers that was all the more enhanced by her innocence. "It's always been a place for contemplation, so I ventured there to think hard upon my position and I found there my answer. I shall not sell Hambly Hall, not even part of it. Tomorrow, I'll start work on a plan to improve production and perhaps see toward new methods. We shall stay here always, dearest."

"I'm so happy, Preston. You belong here, as do I."

"My dear," I said, kissing her cheek.

We stood on the terrace in silence, each communing in our own way. I had no doubt she was relieved to maintain the richness of our present position and also happy with my new resolve. She need never know that it was a lowly gardener fucking his lord and master to newfound ecstasy that carried the day—and would continue to carry it.

As I slipped an arm around her waist, I decided to retreat to my dressing room after supper, wrap my cock in the soiled linen, and have myself off while thinking on Doyle's prick going at me. I'd not need the walking stick any longer. Nor would Sylvia need give way to my growing desire. I issued a chuckle, and she looked at me. "A new chapter for us," I declared, finding the decadence of a gardener's cock enhanced by the presence of my wife. Such an arrangement was madness, yet it brought more satisfaction than I'd known for some time. My prick stirred as if to agree.

# FINNIAS LAREDO

## Alex Stitt

F innias Laredo. Unusual name. Spanish paternity? And more
than punctual. I wasn't expecting you 'til this evening."

"I arrived yesterday, my Lord, to survey the outlying estates."

"Whatever for, man?" Young Master Fletcher cut in, inter-
rupting his father's stolid inquisition. "If you are to be my valet,
you would receive a full tour of the grounds."

At this I paused. Young Master Fletcher was a narrowly built,
college-educated man with the rapt eyes of an academic—and he
looked on me with the fondest curiosity. His previous valet had
dressed him since he was old enough to attend a recital without
fidgeting. Yet when Young Master Fletcher left for Oxford, his
wizened valet was pastured out.

Now graduate alumni, Master Fletcher had returned to his
father's estate in knickerbockers, high socks, and the blue and
white scarf of his home-away-from-home team. Immediately,
his mother had insisted on a new hand-servant. Ordinarily he
wouldn't have taken to it, yet both father and son humored the

consumptive lady of the house while breath was still in her. The whole estate was dark with expectancy, that much was told without telling, and not two moments before my arrival the Young Master had been weighted by the gravity of it. Now his eyes were aglow, for nowhere on my curriculum vitae did it mention my age, and the thought of having a chum of equitable speed seemed to excite him.

"Forgive my impertinence, my Lords, but a valet without proper comprehension of his master's property, propriety and community standing, is about as useful as a ledger without a pen. Educated men are so because they educate themselves."

"Well said," Young Master Fletcher beamed, arising to clap me on the back. "Well, I'm satisfied. Are you, Father?"

"A Spaniard, though?" He squinted, his beard bristling with the thought of it.

"By name and hair certainly," the Young Master wagered, "but Laredo is as true an Englishmen as you or I. I'm sure of it. Tell me Laredo, where were you born?"

"Camberwell."

"Worse than a Spaniard," Lord Fletcher groaned, "a *Londoner*. Fine, be done with it. Report to Mr. Gurner, and God save your stitching hand. My son's always losing buttons. The finest education and the boy still can't master clothes!"

Packing the funnel, I slid the bristle out of the barrel and handed off the rifle.

"Wherever did you learn to load in Camberwell, Laredo?"

"While serving as a kitchen hand at Moorland House, my Lord. I was young. Mr. Aterly used to take the gardener and I to the country."

"And what do you think of the country now that you have a man's eyes?" he asked, lying in the grass with the gun propped on his elbow. He was a long, sinewy fellow, more skin than muscle, which made his tweed Norfolk jacket appear tighter than it was if only for the sheer lack of fabric.

"With a man's eyes I see nothing but opportunity," I returned kindly, relying on compassion as currency.

With kindness I'd bought my way out of the kitchens to a stint as Mr. Aterly's coachman, then a post as Mr. Ippington's valet, warranting enough recommendations for the Fletcher estate. Yet sensitivity as a device requires preemptive consideration—a life-saving cup of tea at a champagne soiree, a pre-selected gift for their lady in waiting, or perhaps a prepared suit predicting an otherwise unpredictable change in schedule. And when at last they realized how impeccable I was, I would make my observation.

"My Lord?"

"Yes, Laredo?" Master Fletcher asked, leaning slowly into the stock.

"I see your game."

"As do I, Laredo."

"Not the pheasant, my Lord."

"Unless you happen upon a lion in the heather of Cornwall, I haven't the faintest idea what you're on about." One click, one boom, and one sulfurous cloud of smoke later, and we saw three pheasants scatter. "Blast! Well, fine, what is it Laredo? What game are you on about?"

"You honestly don't see it, do you?"

"Her Majesty's Lion? No more than I see her unicorn! Now spit it out. What don't I see?"

"How sad you are."

"Excuse me? A poor shot I may be, Laredo, but I'm not about to weep on the earth over the matter."

"You smile so willingly and so bravely that you don't think anyone notices. But I do. There's a kindness in you. I saw it last week when Lady Armice dined with your father."

"Lady Armice would wrest my mother's wedding ring from her grave if she could. But honestly, Laredo, you've been my valet for three months now. You should know me well enough not to launch into psychoanalysis. You have about as much chance with that as you have theosophy."

"A balm, my Lord?"

"For my soul, Laredo? The vicar said it all after the funeral. What more could you add?"

"For your hand. You burnt it on the muzzle."

"It's only soot."

"I'm glad of it."

"Are you, Laredo? I imagine you would much rather heal me if you had the chance."

"If I can restitch your suit, why not apply the same remedy to your smile?"

"Well, if grief were as easy to mend as a pair of trousers, I'd let you and make a tailor of Mr. Freud."

"It's all about finding the right thread, I'm sure."

"Are all Spaniards such romantics?" He smirked over his gun.

"Only the ones from Camberwell."

The carriage jostled, as carriages are wont to do, yet that wasn't why Young Master Fletcher bit his lip. He was trying to silence himself. The driver kept asking questions, causing him to answer in short, sharp bursts.

Seven months in service and two weeks in Edinburgh had brought us to a Scottish pub, where, not wanting to seem brash or moneyed, I was introduced as a colleague. A leveling of title had leveled us in his bedroom, with the age-old aphrodisiac of Edwardian sex: bourbon.

Now we were riding home with two bottles of Speyside Single Malt, my master's gloves pawing clumsily at my hair. He would never kiss a man in the Grace of God, but by God's graces he let me kiss him everywhere else—so long as I obeyed the ritual. Whispering about the wiles of Scottish women, I would start to lean, shifting topics from breasts to capitulation until I could almost brush his neck with my lips. At which point he would present his hand for me to kiss, requiring that I kneel.

As his valet, I knew every button and buckle, having sewn and polished them all, and they held no mysteries back. Like an illusionist conjuring off his clothes, I slid his trousers away, revealing his drunk, half-sure erection. Aroused by the prospect of arousal, it slid lazily against his leg while my tentative kisses climbed his thigh. He would never fully harden until I took him into my mouth. He tensed, his eyes shut tight for the shame and pleasure of it.

During my first attempt in Scotland, I swore he might strike me, yet I swallowed his indignation until he was empty of all save joy. Never had he felt so released, and so a valet became a colleague in orgasmic collusion, tossing him against the sheets in ways he always wished his college chums might.

And now we were on our way home, back to the estate, and time was running out.

The carriage rumbled over the cobbles. His eyes closed. His pride swayed.

Heat coursed and quivered to the arrow-shaped head of his cock, and I smiled at his surname as some little joke took me. Being a man of youthful spirit, his scrotum tightened against his shaft, expanding and retracting every time I licked my way to the base. Setting my teeth against his skin, as if feigning a bite, I stroked and palmed the head, which flushed from purple to scarlet—royal colors to my mind.

His hips bucked. He let out a sound part grunt, part silent roar, mouth agape, hands pawing at the ceiling.

The driver apologized for the pothole.

Young Masters, spoiled and benevolent alike, are always of an incorrigible nature. Raised with silver spoon, they're taught to aspire for gold, making self-reliance their highest achievement. It is better in their minds to have all good men—or at the very least all good businessmen—remain in their pocket, yet whether they keep them there via favor or debt is an entirely Machiavellian matter. As such, few Young Masters understand the reciprocity of this relationship because they have never been able to rely on empathy. Expectancy alone raised them like a wet nurse, pulling them into the future, but few had ever pushed them from behind.

"Laredo? My pipe."

"It's under your seat, my Lord."

"How did you know I'd come here to the balcony?"

"Well, after Miss Rowinoak made a fool of you downstairs, I knew you would find a solitary place so as not to spoil your father's wedding."

"But why not the smoking room, or my chamber, or the orangery?"

"Because it's a summer night, it's going to rain and the leeward side of the house will protect your phenomenal view of the pavilion. Slatted pergolas are poor cover. Should I inform Mr. Gurner to fetch umbrellas?"

"There is," he said, ignoring my question, "a risk you may have soaked my tobacco."

"It *was* under your seat, my Lord."

Smiling momentarily, he withdrew the parquet box and removed his pipe.

"I wasn't going to invest," he said, his long fingers pinching shreds of tobacco. "I just couldn't. Miss Rowinoak is more than adventurous with her money, as she would be with mine! Father calls it loose cannon spending, and for once the old bombardier is right."

Master Fletcher never smoked much, but he smoked often, his usage precise and gingerly. He did not ram his pipe full, as did his father, instead being smooth and quick with his motions. The bowl was white ivory, which he kept unusually immaculate. It was the only object I was forbidden to polish. He said he took a pleasure in it himself.

"I just couldn't invest," he sighed again, "and I couldn't stay down there. Her entrepreneurial talents are divine and her gusto is the kind I aspire to in myself—I could marry a woman like that, Laredo—but she asks too much."

"There are cheaper women in Piccadilly, my Lord."

"This is not London, man, and Miss Rowinoak is no whore!"

"A point you chose to make second."

"But you're right."

"My Lord?"

"There are cheaper women in Piccadilly."

Pipe in mouth, head in hands, he threw himself back in his chair—his dramatic recline borrowed from Simone, Oscar Wilde's brokenhearted lead in the *Florentine Tragedy*. We had seen the play together at Plymouth's Theatre Royal, yet I was more enraptured by my master's smile than anything an Irish dandy could compose.

"She's bold and brave and she would have us sink a fortune into where? *Kirkuk*? The Kaiser may have lost his grip, but the Turkish Petroleum Company? In bed with the Dutch? And the Americans? We could be rich but...it gambles everything."

Slowly, the first pattering rain stole over the roof. A flare illuminated his sharp cheeks from below, and, with a deep exhale, wreaths of smoke poured over his lips.

He had no idea how much I loved him.

"It is true what they say, my Lord. Good men and good businessmen are poor synonyms. Perhaps it's best if your next partner *is* a woman."

"It's not that I do not trust her gender, Laredo; it's that I do not trust my mind when I'm around her. My incentives are my own implacable handicap."

"Do you trust your mind around me, my Lord?"

"I said implacable, Laredo. You're impeccable. If half the men at Oxford were as sharp as you, I would have some faith in the world's future."

"Then would you permit me a question? Though it may be more of a memory to you now."

"Of course," he puffed again. "But only if you have one of those foul roll-ups of yours. You leave me standing when I smoke alone."

Moving to the rail beside, I unclasped the plated case in my pocket. I had hoped not to smoke my own supply, but the groom's cigars did not extend to me, nor currently his embarrassing arse of a son. The failed Rowinoak courtship was discomforting enough, but Lord Fletcher was beginning to suspect his young Toby of bohemian ideals he himself had no name for.

"Do you remember the first day of hunting?" I lit up, tossing the match at the pavilion. "In the spring? I had asked you a question."

"Not particularly, no. I'm sure there were many questions answered and misspoken. If I told you something incorrectly then I am sorry."

"Why apologize, my Lord?"

"Because I may have just ruined my future standings as an eligible negotiator in both love and business, and I would apologize to a housecat if it meowed at me now."

"I asked if you could see how truly sad you are."

"Damn you, Laredo!" he growled, all smoke and heartache. "You call my intended a whore *and* mock me for my pathetic attempts at love? Give me one, but not the other."

"Forgive me, Toby, I was being literal. Simply put, I can't believe how much sorrow you subject yourself too. You are so kind, and yet you restrain yourself with grief. Miss Rowinoak is just your shadow walking in front of you, but she isn't your only one."

"Your smile is too sincere, Laredo."

"Give her your heart, my Lord, and your money and your betrothal. I only ask for your honesty."

"If that were the honest truth then why am I so cautious of your laxity? I would say you've forgotten yourself, but this is really your way, isn't it, Laredo? You are genuinely earnest."

"Shall I prepare you for bed, my Lord?"

"I know it's your job, man, but the party is not yet over."

"I agree," I nodded. "But shall I prepare you for bed, my Lord?"

Silver-backed mirrors have always been the secret to beauty. As time goes on, their fading metals present gentler and gentler reflections, until all that remains is a blended echo akin to our memories of youth. As it was, the Young Master's standup mirror had remained in the family for more than a century. He said it came from the Mediterranean.

"—which is why I love to see you in it, Laredo," he sighed as I set his cuff links in their box. "With you, in this mirror, I could imagine us boarding at some Catalonian inn—sailing every day. Clear waters. Clear skies. Nothing like this."

Outside, the rain let loose, moving everyone in. The musicians had relocated to the main hall, and now every corridor was abuzz with maids fetching dry towels and warm tea.

"I have never been to Spain, my Lord."

When I slid my fingers under the collar of his jacket, he automatically raised his shoulders, freeing his arms of the coat via our intimate if puppeted routine. He ruled me by occupation, adoration, and secrecy of sexuality, yet one tap to the inside of his ankle and he would raise his foot like a show pony. Certainly, I was the one to remove his shoes, inflating his sense of benevolence, but one tap to the underside of his arm and he would turn for me again, losing his confidence to propinquity. Face-to-face, I undid his ivory shirt buttons. He had already unwound his tie.

"Laredo?" he asked as I pulled his shirt open. My eyes were downcast. He blinked once at his own chest. "Why do you make so much of this?"

"So much of you, my Lord?" I asked, skimming a flat hand across his stomach. "Because you are beautiful and kind, two sentiments rarely met."

"A rarity in Camberwell, perhaps?"

"To one like I, yes."

"Like you? A Spaniard's bastard?" he said, holding his breath so as not to seem so drunk, which was adorable in a way. I had measured his glass deliberately, and we were both aware of it.

"A sinner, my Lord."

Sighing, he looked back to the mirror.

"Forgive me, Laredo. I'm bitter."

"If you're bitter then I blame the caviar—for it's a flavor I would never associate with you."

"And *you* say *I'm* beautiful and kind? Well, if you say it then it must be so because I'm not about to make a liar of you. Oh

Lord, there are those eyes again! Were you but a woman I would walk you downstairs and steal this soggy wedding."

"Perhaps it's less the caviar and more the wine," I mused, stepping away to hang his shirt in the wardrobe.

"Come back, Laredo," he said, his suspenders dangling free about his waist. "Don't chill yourself to me. I'm sorry. I'll...I'll grant you anything. Would you have a raise? It's done. Your own horse? Have your pick."

"Beware, my Lord, I am the sort to wish for more wishes."

"And how many would satisfy you?"

"Two, actually," I said, returning to hold his gaze. He didn't even realize I had his belt until it was slung over my shoulder.

"So name it."

"I want a night like Edinburgh. I want a night where I don't have to go back to the servant's quarters. I want you to keep me 'til morning."

"Yes...but the house is very busy tonight."

"All the more noise to hide us."

"And your other wish?" he swallowed, having lost his breath.

"My Lord, it occurs to me that for over a year I've dressed you, redressed you, and undressed you...and yet I've never undressed myself."

"I do remember the lakeside, Laredo. We were the only ones for miles."

"No, my Lord. Removing one's clothes is not as couth as *undressing*."

"Then," he gasped again, "by all means, man."

First I found the Young Master a chair. He was a proximity-fucker—my little term for circumstantial homosexuals who clung so tight so as not to see themselves penetrating another man. Mr. Ippington was my first prototype for this. With his face in my hair and his eyes shut, he copulated with his own prude imagination. But the Young Master had different reasons for drawing me in.

Unlike Mr. Ippington, he didn't reject my body. If anything, he jealously admired it, embarrassed as he was of his own ecto-morphic frame. He was smooth and delicate with the faintest and fairest hair, granting his body an even whiter sheen. This was the truth of his faded mirror. He was a ghostly boy who hated to look upon himself. Even now he attempted to cross his legs so as not to notice his own aroused reflection.

An exhibition would not be easy for him.

Untying my cravat, I loosened my collar and stepped out of my shoes with surprising ease. Blinking at my trickery, he watched me balance one bare foot on his knee. I wore no socks, a sacrilege to my Master and his ankle garters.

"And no undershirt, either? By the way you're so under-dressed I might suspect you predicted Miss Rowinoak would gut my dignity."

"No, my Lord," I smiled, unbuttoning the last of my shirt. "Nothing so oracular. Miss Rowinoak will evade your chamber 'til you're betrothed, so no matter how you imagined it you were always going to end tonight alone...with me."

"And you assumed I would be in the mood for your games?"

"As with all drunk men on the wedding night of other men."

Dipping the shoulders of my shirt, I let it bundle about my chest with womanly languor. He needed the little things, though not for illusion's sake, since I could never be mistaken as a woman. Hard work in kitchen and stable had made my body gaunt but hard, and like so many peasants when compared with gentry, I had more definition than my master. Yet I posed so delicately to entreat his masculinity. Having shod horses and carried wine casks, I could break him so easily, a reality which would deflate his ego and his love of me if he ever realized it. No, he didn't desire me to be a woman—he desired himself to be a man. Sliding my foot off his knee, I stood over his thigh, my shirt hooked to my wrists like a low-lying cape. Teasing the tongue of my belt, I slid the leather strap out of its buckle. Hypnotized, his breeches tightened, though we were locked at an impasse, my legs astride his. Pulling my belt, one notch at a time, I had him watch and wait. He wanted to push me onto his four-post bed, but this was a demonstration.

As my waistline dipped, my master saw no undergarments of any kind—only muscle where my stomach V-lined to the last row of buttons between us. He looked down at them. I looked down at him, licked my thumb, and trailed it along my front as if somehow that magic motion were the key.

When it comes to trousers, the largest button, the master button, straightens the pleat together, yet it's easily disarmed with a press and flick. All buttons thereafter offer little resistance, giving way with ample pressure to the fabric. To my master's eye, I barely touched my groin, and my trousers peeled open of their own accord.

Half-dressed, with my shirt draped behind me still, I thumbed my belt loops and pulled slowly down. A short crop of black hair outlined my pelvis. As a boy I'd been shaved habitually to stave off lice. Yet as a man I'd kept up the act with a straight razor, wishing nothing to distract from my cock.

While his penis was a spring-loaded surprise, all short one minute and all girth the next, mine maintained its size whether I was excited or no. Eighteen centimeters swung down as I bent forward. I couldn't tell if he was admiring or comparing or both, so I stole his attention with a kiss, tilting his chin up with another directive tap.

Yet, when my tongue touched his, a thirst stole over him. My knees buckled, my cock tightened, and I collapsed on his lap, my trousers still bunched awkwardly between my legs. Riding his knee, my spare hand slipped through the pleat of his breeches, fanned wide, and popped all his buttons with one go. I'd sewn them all before, and I'd be glad to sew them again, just to see that startle in his eyes.

My jaw slackened when I saw that arrow-headed friend of mine. He was tight—excited and frustrated by the night's affairs—and when I gripped, I felt the blood constrict and swell. Sliding higher on his lap, I smacked his shaft with mine like a fencer striking a challenge. In turn, he reached between my legs, grabbing the base of my cock behind the scrotum to pull everything up together. This was his leash.

Pushing back his chair to stand, he held me fast as gravity stole the rest of my trousers. My shirt I left on with forethought.

Bedside, he laid into my lips with kisses no woman would ever respect him for. He licked the underside of my top lip with a gluttony wealthy boys of his nature were both famous for and famous for hiding. He wanted all of me and he didn't know where to start.

Releasing his lock on my genitals, his hand slid tentatively down the length of my perineum, which he smoothed with his fingers as if fantasizing about Miss Rowinoak. My master had never actually slept with a woman and neither had I, yet for entirely different reasons. Biting his lip, I guided his hand farther back, returning him to the moment. Pushing my cheeks apart, he lifted me up to the balls of my feet, before toppling me onto his duvet.

Legs open, my erection arched against my front, a curve mimicked by my spine. His fingers pressed in search of a way in, and he bit my stomach and kissed my skin and spread my thighs wider.

"My Lord," I uttered, and when he looked up I nodded to his goose-feather pillows. Climbing forward, bringing his hips up to my chest, he discovered a small jar of lard. An epiphany caught him as to my usefulness, my utilization, and my love, but he didn't have time to linger as I plunged his cock into my mouth.

Doubling forward with his weight on his elbows, he thrust into the back of my throat, driving his pelvis like a jockey on horseback. I could suck on a canter, but had to open wide to let him gallop—less I choke on his speed. A violence took him, and he grabbed my hair as if I might escape. I'd never dream of it, though my legs thrashed and crossed akimbo.

He fucked my mouth as if imagining some cruel vengeance, fulfilling an act he would administer on every rotter who'd ever done him wrong. And I? I gagged on my own salivating excitement. My young master wasn't a sadist nor a Parisian fetishist, but he was virile and in need of proving himself, one way or another.

Withdrawing, he stepped off the bed with his newfound jar. I heard the lid roll on the floor. I smelled the faint waft of grease. Then I felt two fingers, slick and wide and terribly fast. I lost my breath and shot bolt upright, only to find his hand cupping my hip and keeping me down.

Willowy as he was, his fingers were long and his palm was wide, giving him both reach and grip of my body, inside and out. My sphincter relaxed around his knuckles as a quiet, pleasurable ache shuddered within me. Throwing my head back, I gasped and drank in air. His motions slowed as he slid in and out—as if remembering his sensitive valet. I relaxed, as did his smile, and he pulled out momentarily.

A Fletcher by occupation is a man who feathers arrows, while a Fletcher by name is a man who never misses his target.

Gripping my hips with both hands, I felt his arrow-headed cock press my arse. Streamlined and smooth, he drove in with no resistance save a heavy sigh on both our parts, and no assistance save an aspiration of mine to take him all at once. And I did, but slower than I expected. Previously, with my lips on his prick, he'd forgotten me, but we were face-to-face now, my legs hitched, his thrust a tease to us both.

His undone breeches brushed against my buttocks every time he pushed forward, and as he gained momentum I rolled back onto my shoulders, leaving my feet high in the air. Sweat trickled along his jaw, and when I tried to wrap my arms behind his head, he shoved me down, pinning me by the only thing left clothed—my sleeved wrists.

A hard bang hit me in two places at once. The first was deep inside where his cock could shove no more, followed instantly by his pelvis spanking against my arse.

Again he galloped—that terrible, wonderful ache expanding within me—and I cried out, no doubt alerting the guests of the house, though my mind and my rectum cared not for the opinions of others. I felt an opening, a rush riding hard to the very depths. My erection bounced helplessly against my front as I gasped and moaned and gasped again.

I felt him building, yet before the summit he pulled out, flipped me over, and grabbed my twisted shirt like a set of reins. With my knees down and my rump in the air, he pulled my arms out from under me, plowing me facedown into the comforters. As my pain succumbed to pleasure, he transformed from jockey to charioteer, leaning back to lengthen each pull and push in rhythm—from hilt to tip to hilt. His testicles were tight and retracted, but mine swung free with a weight and tension of their own.

Granting slack to my shirt, he allowed me to paw and claw

myself up, curving my spine and rounding my buttocks. I rocked into him as he pounded into me, and for a rebellious moment we warred over direction until he fucked hard enough to remind me of my duty. Speeding to a heavy, banging pace, I swore the head of my own untouched cock would pop. It was all I could do to brace myself so as not to collapse us both.

His cock flexed with his heartbeat. I cried out. He wrapped his arms about my torso. Physically carrying me up, he lifted my weight to shove me down one last time. Hitting some indeterminable heaven, a searing shot convulsed through me. His orgasm burst into mine—spurting across my thighs and his pillows as a shaking, twitching wetness consumed us.

Perspiring and sweating, we locked in a wrestler's pose, his arms clasped across my chest, my hands clawing at the back of his head. I felt his come filling me up and trickling out and covering us both. I felt shaky and out of breath and dizzy with stamina.

Not losing a centimeter to postcoital relax, he stiffened his cock in me, causing my own to throb.

Sitting atop him, I caved in exhaustion, leaving my master free to fuck and slide at his leisure. Yet, as he peered over my shoulder, he fondled my now-tightened balls, pulling and groping as I had seen rich men absently juggle a money purse. It hurt and satisfied at the same time, and as I succumbed he slowly poured out of me.

Wiping off on the sheets—oblivious of the world that served to clean up his—he turned me over, my own come beneath me, his own propriety beneath him.

"My Lord?"

"Recompense, Laredo," he whispered, and for the first time in our companionship he serviced me.

Still in the throes of my last climax, I writhed—agonized

by sensitivity and tortured by amateur vigor. He sucked hard to prove himself, but it felt like a punishment, and when he saw my teeth clench, he relaxed his effort. I felt bad because I knew he wanted to thank me, and at the same time I knew I'd be unable to come again. Until, that was, he remembered his valet's weakness.

That caving emptiness re-expanded as he fingered me again. While his head bobbed up and down like a wet sheath, his fingers reached back. My postorgasmic chills rewound to the present, and I offered myself up to him. I barely moved—I barely could—and as his lips slipped back and forth over the crown of my head, he twisted his hand to fit in three fingers. The lard was still slick on all sides, and so three fingers quickly became four. He could not possibly make a fist of it less he desired to kill me, but four bunched fingers spread me wide.

I shook—my jaw agape as I came into the back of his mouth. He gagged, white dribbling over his chin, yet as he hacked I came again, his bunched fingers still pummeling and widening. Out of fluid but not out of pleasure, my voice returned with tears, and I cried aloud. For a moment I thought I'd detached my body, and when the pummeling ceased I fell back into a husk more animal than man. I could have died then and there, and been happy to leave my carnal carcass behind, but in truth I was more alive than ever.

A shadow moved to my stead. Again he wiped his hands on the sheets and stuffed his now-limp cock back into his breeches. He poured himself a bourbon. I poured myself some composure.

"Would you," I paused, still trying to think, "like me to leave, my Lord?"

"Why, Laredo?" He turned, wild-eyed and wide awake. "It's not yet dawn."

Breakfast was lavish, Lady Armice-cum-Fletcher sparing none of her newfound husband's expense. The whole staff was required, I myself serving orange juice to Miss Rowinoak when she requested Toby and I escort her to the depot. There was to be no argument, and while the carriage was quick, the ride was awkwardly genial, their candor guarded by etiquette.

"—and I, for one, am glad of you, Laredo," she said, bidding farewell as the steam whistled from her boarding train. "The boy needs a little bohemian in his life. Oh, don't be so coy, Toby. Buggery is a gentleman's sport. I just didn't realize one needed a cock to pry your purse. Shame really, we could have made such a fortune in Kirkuk."

Flabbergasted, Toby idled. The train departed. I assumed heartache, but on reaching our carriage he burst into laughter— a bachelor again.

Summer was on us and the flowers were out. Sighing, I bit my lip, fidgeting restlessly in my seat. Gulping air, I gripped the curtain and subdued my noise. The ride back was short, but the ritual took time, and our excitable conversation didn't hit its peak until we were halfway home.

Gravel popped under the wheels. The carriage stopped. I heard the guests departing, and Lord Fletcher seeing them off. Hurriedly, I buckled my belt. The coachman opened the door. Sunlight flooded the carriage.

"Toby," Lord Fletcher blinked. "What are you doing on your knees?"

"Nothing, Father," Toby smiled and swallowed. "I just... dropped a button, that's all."

# FINSLOE

## Xavier Axelson

I knew I loved Master Bryden Massingham when, as boys, he kissed me in the broom closet. He'd stolen a custard tart from the kitchen and entreated me to share his spoils. The tart broke apart, and we slurped custard from our hands.

"You got custard on your chin!" I laughed.

"I do?" Bryden swiped his tongue along his bottom lip. "How about now?"

I shook my head.

He leaned in close. "Get it for me."

I smelled sweet custard on his breath.

"Go on, before we're caught!"

I lifted my finger and brushed it against his chin. Our eyes met. He smiled. I blushed.

He came closer, and when our lips touched, I closed my eyes. The kiss lasted a moment but it haunted me like a hungry ghost. I wanted more, ached to be alone with him. Whenever our eyes met, he smiled as though our secret pleased him.

I'd been in service a year by then. My pa served as butler at Massingham Place. When my ma took sick with fever and died the winter before, he pleaded with Lord and Lady Massingham to oblige his only son.

I did chores, scrambled out of the way of cooks, footmen and maids, but mostly I played with Master Bryden.

The day before Master Bryden left for university, he came to the garret bedroom I shared with Pa and Mr. Prewitt, the underbutler. Collins, the footman, had an even tinier room that adjoined ours, both visible from either side of the space allotted.

I couldn't sleep, and stared at the shadows on the ceiling and listened to Pa snore.

I hadn't heard Bryden enter but smelled bay rum. He started wearing the scent when he received a bottle as a gift on his eighteenth birthday. My heart pounded every time I caught a trace of it in the air.

His hand slid under the rough cotton sheet. When his hand grazed my thigh, I trembled. Pa snored louder.

My thoughts ranged from fear to disbelief and excited terror. I looked over at Mr. Prewitt and hoped he was asleep.

Master Bryden's hand crept inside my drawers and fondled my cock. It stiffened in the wisdom of a sure hand. I turned my face from the shadows on the ceiling and breathed heavily against the flat pillow beneath my head. My cock grew wet, slick with urgent expectancy. His hand stroked faster until I whimpered. I couldn't hold back. My body shook, quivered, undulated until I cried out, my cock ejaculating. Drenched like a sailor tossed from his ship, I was sprayed with the hot, pungent stuff. I sighed as it trickled down my thighs.

It all ended as suddenly as it had begun.

Mr. Prewitt didn't move. My pa continued to snore.

The next morning, Master Bryden was gone.

Two years later, just short of my twenty-first birthday, Pa died in service to the Massingham family. Mr. Prewitt took Pa's place as head butler, Collins moved up to underbutler, while I moved up from page to footman.

"Mrs. Pearce." Mr. Prewitt stood before a splendidly laid servant's table. "You have outdone yourself!"

I looked over the platter of roasted meat, steamed vegetables and Mrs. Pearce's crowning glory: a towering almond sponge. Mrs. Pearce beamed while Mr. Prewitt lifted the carving knife and fork.

Collins leaned close and whispered, "You hear Master Bryden be coming home?"

"Piss off!" I hissed and pushed him away.

"Finsloe!" Mr. Prewitt and Mrs. Pearce glared my way.

I lowered my eyes. "Pardon me, Mr. Prewitt, Mrs. Pearce."

"What is it requires you to interrupt our meal?"

"Nothing, Mr. Prewitt."

Collins snickered.

"Collins?" Mr. Prewitt's voice went up a notch.

"Nothing, Mr. Prewitt."

"You boys are always up to no good," Mrs. Pearce added for good measure.

"Right you are, Mrs. Pearce," Mr. Prewitt agreed.

"If you please, Mr. Prewitt," Collins interjected, "it wasn't entirely Finsloe's fault; I told him something unexpected."

Mrs. Pearce snorted with derision. "And what might this something be, eh? The cow jumped over the moon, did it?"

Linney, the scullery maid, let out a high-pitched squeal of laughter and received a pinch from Mary Ann, the kitchen maid.

"Maybe the fork ran away with the spoon!" rejoined Lavender, who served as ladies' maid.

"Yes, tell us Collins," Mr. Prewitt commanded, "before our meal is spoiled with your tomfoolery."

"I hear Master Bryden be coming home," blurted Collins.

"Cheek!" Mrs. Pearce shrieked.

"And where did you hear this news, Collins?" Mr. Prewitt asked as he regained the fork and knife and carved the meat.

"I heard it from a couple of reliable sources." Collins bit back a smile. He enjoyed the chaos the news caused.

"Your sources," Mr. Prewitt continued after passing the plate to Mrs. Pearce, who served the vegetables, "are ill-advised. I've heard no such news, and I insist everyone at this table refrain from spreading such nonsense." He stared hard at Collins. "Is that clear?"

Collins hesitated long enough to create an uncomfortably tense silence. "Yes, Mr. Prewitt."

"Good. Now Finsloe, shall I serve you, or would you like to at least pretend to do your job?"

I jumped from my seat and took my place by Mrs. Pearce, who handed me the full plate. I stared at the food in bewilderment.

*Master Bryden...coming home,* I thought to myself.

"Finsloe!"

Mr. Prewitt's beady black eyes bore into me. "For God's sake, lad, serve the food!"

Polishing silver, opening and closing doors, serving and clearing: the day went by in a blur.

I couldn't stop thinking of Master Bryden. What was he like now? Where had he been? Gossip swirled around his name until I no longer knew truth from myth. Still, I knew the truth of his touch and hungered to feel it again.

"Finsloe!"

I was helping Linney move a large stack of heavy pots when Mr. Prewitt summoned me.

"Lord, I thought I had it hard!" Linney exclaimed. "He's got you jumpin' like a pup all day long."

I shrugged. "Don't hardly notice anymore." I wiped my hands and left her to the pots.

Mr. Prewitt, along with Mrs. Pearce, awaited me. Tom, the baker's son, stood behind them, a sack of bread at his feet.

Mr. Prewitt looked disapprovingly at the large, awkward man who fumbled with the sack of loaves, nearly avoiding a collision with Mary Ann.

"Look sharp, my girl!" Mrs. Pearce shouted and then clucked her tongue.

Mr. Prewitt rolled his eyes. "Finsloe, show Tom to the pantry and help put away the week's bread."

"Yes, Mr. Prewitt." I stepped back to give Tom and the bag of bread enough space to pass.

Mrs. Pearce shook her head as Tom lumbered forward and knocked a sack of flour over. He'd spun around to apologize further when he stepped on Mrs. Pearce's toes.

"Get out!" she shrieked and hopped about, until Mary Ann rushed her to a nearby stool.

I hurried him from the room. The sound of angry voices followed us until we reached the relative seclusion of the pantry.

He let out a relieved sigh and put the sack down by his feet. "Don't know how you do it."

I crouched down and cleared an area for the loaves. "Do what?" The pantry smelled of grain, yeast and flour. I'd be covered in white dust by the time we were through.

"Manage not to trip over every maid and man in this blasted place!"

I smirked. "I keep my head on my work and my own affairs. Now hand over that bread."

"Yessir." He hauled the sack up and over to me. His dark eyes surveyed the well-stocked shelves. "How's things?"

I thought of the news about Master Bryden. "Same as usual." I removed bread from the sack and stacked it in the designated cupboards.

Tom reached over and put a large hand on my shoulder. "You all right?" His rough-hewn face creased with concern.

"Yeah, fine. Just a bit tired, I guess."

Tom squeezed my shoulder. "Been a while since I seen you alone."

Tom and I shared a friendship forged by the secret knowledge of each other's desires. He had revealed himself to me months earlier when I accidentally brushed against him, his erection responding in kind. Since then, we had shared many clandestine moments. I enjoyed the feel of his muscular, ox-like bulk against my body. His crooked smile lifted my spirits.

"Miss that pretty cock of yours." He grinned and placed a fat baguette between his legs. "You miss mine?"

I grabbed the loaf and yanked it from him. "You're crazy."

"Am I?" Tom crouched down and leaned against me so I could smell his earthy scent. "I been hearing things on the street, you know."

"I bet." I took another loaf and wedged it between several rolls.

"Some say Master Bryden be returning."

I looked at him. "Cheap gossip is all that is."

"I don't care either way." His hand slid from my shoulder and searched between my legs.

"What are you doing?"

"Delivering bread, sir." His tongue licked the edge of my neck.

I tried to resist, but lost my balance and fell back against several large sacks of grain. Tom took advantage of my position and got on top of me.

"What if someone comes in," I protested.

"Ain't no one comin' but you," Tom replied, then kissed me. I yielded to his wet, fat tongue as my body sunk deeper into the grain sacks. Tom undid his trousers, tugged his balls free and pushed his thick cock forward. "I wants that sweet mouth a' yours!"

I lowered my chin and nuzzled the uncut tip of Tom's cock with my lips. The skin retracted and pushed forth a swollen, wet head. I smelled the pungent maleness of Tom's crotch. Everything I longed for seemed to be part of that smell. I opened my mouth and took Tom's swollen cock into it.

Tom moaned as his prick probed the back of my throat. "That's a lad," he urged.

I sucked Tom deeper. Saliva spilled from my mouth and slicked my hands. Tom lifted his hips and forced himself farther down my throat. I tasted salt, and Tom's flood of come made me choke. Hot embarrassment overwhelmed me as I involuntarily swallowed. I beat my cock until my head swam, and reluctantly let go when Tom's hand replaced my own and his powerful strokes urged my own release. He bent down in time to catch the first spurt of come on his face and then greedily took my spewing prick into his mouth. I bit back a moan and finally grabbed a small roll from the shelf above us before jamming it inside my mouth.

When it stopped, he looked up at me and let my cock slip from his mouth. "Sweet as puddin' pie." He licked his lips.

I took the bit-through roll from my mouth and tossed it at him.

Tom caught the roll and ate the remainder. "Come on then."

He stood and offered his arm.

I declined it and steadied myself against the bread cabinet.

Tom yanked his pants up and wiped at his stomach with the empty bread sack. "Best be goin' then." He put his hand on my shoulder. "Only good thing about this job is takin' a bit a pleasure where you find it." Tom left the pantry but looked back at me, smiled his crooked smile, then disappeared down the hallway.

After the Massinghams retired for the night, the staff settled around the kitchen. I assisted Linney, serving hot cocoa.

Mrs. Pearce stared anxiously into the dwindling embers of the kitchen hearth. "You don't think there's any truth in what Collins said, do you Mr. Prewitt?"

"Not a bit, Mrs. Pearce," Mr. Prewitt insisted.

I remained silent and finished my cocoa. "I'll take myself to bed, if you don't mind, Mr. Prewitt."

Mr. Prewitt nodded. "Yes, Finsloe, see you in the morning."

I bowed and removed myself to the garret.

Our room smelled of Collins's lime aftershave. He'd be out most of the night, sleep a few hours, then sneak a nap during the next day's labors.

I undressed and got into bed. My mind, full from all that had happened, struggled to find sleep, but I must have drifted off because I awoke to find Collins sitting on the edge of his bed.

"Collins?"

He didn't move or look up from his hands. "It's Master Bryden." Collins lifted his head. "Found him drunk at the pub. He'd been in a brawl and was stumblin' around like a fool. Had to practically carry him home."

I bolted upright. "Master Bryden, he's here?"

"Fast asleep in his bed, thanks to me." Collins undressed.

"Bloody fool. What he's doing drinkin' at a place like that, beats me."

My stomach churned with nervous excitement. "Do the lord and lady know?"

"No, I managed to get him to bed without anyone knowin' the better. But you best be sure the streets'll be buzzin' tomorrow."

"You must tell Mr. Prewitt immediately."

"I'm bloody buggery beat." Collins threw on his nightshirt. "It can wait until morning, for all I care. Besides, Master Bryden will sleep until noon if I know anything." He blew out the lamp and fell into bed.

The next morning I found Collins's bed empty. I rushed to get ready and hurried downstairs to find Mr. Prewitt and Collins at the servant's dining table, locked in conversation. I crept into the kitchen, where Mrs. Pearce and Mary Ann readied the morning meal. Both women seemed tense, and when Mary Ann dropped a spoon and it clattered on the floor, Mrs. Pearce practically sent a toast caddy flying in the air.

"Fool girl!" Mrs. Pearce screamed. "Get out of my kitchen before you're the death of me!"

Mary Ann grabbed the tray she'd prepared with jam, butter and cream for toast and coffee before promptly scattering.

I picked up the spoon. "Everything all right?"

"Is everything all right!" Mrs. Pearce shrieked. "Don't ask me!" She pointed at a stack of plates. "Bring those into the other room and set the table. Don't stand there gaping!"

I left her nervously scraping burnt bits off the toast.

Mr. Prewitt and Collins looked at me when I entered, but didn't speak. Mary Ann and I set the table quietly, and once we were all assembled, Mr. Prewitt stood. Collins removed himself to his spot beside me.

"Before we break fast, I have an announcement." Mr. Prewitt cast his gaze around the table. "Last night, Master Bryden returned home. It appears Mr. Collins was correct." He paused to acknowledge Collins with a nod. "His Lordship and My Lady will be notified when they come down for their morning meal."

Amidst the surprised gasps and shocked faces, Mr. Prewitt continued. "Finsloe, for the time being, you will serve as Master Bryden's valet."

I could feel my body begin to shake, but managed to hold still. "Yes, Mr. Prewitt."

"Bring him a tray once you've finished with your morning duties." He turned his gaze on the kitchen staff. "We will all do our best to accommodate Master Bryden's abrupt arrival. There will be no ill tongue about it inside or outside this house. Is that understood?"

A chorus of "Yes, Mr. Prewitt" ensued.

Once I served everyone, I sat and stared at my toast, unable to eat.

"Now, don't spill," Mrs. Pearce instructed as she placed both a steaming tea and coffee pot on Master Bryden's tray. "He always liked a big breakfast."

"Yes, Mrs. Pearce," I said, then lifted the heavy tray, balancing it on my shoulder as I left the kitchen.

Collins caught up with me. "Mind yourself, Finsloe. I heard Master Bryden's last valet disappeared under mysterious circumstances."

"Get away!" I strode past him and started up the stairs.

Mysterious circumstances! Damned Collins and his gossip!

I halted outside Master Bryden's door. Flashes of memory played with my thoughts. His face, his smile, the way his hands explored and stroked my body…would he even remember?

I knocked, waited and, getting no reply, knocked louder and announced myself.

Nothing. The tray balanced on my shoulder, I leaned in and turned the doorknob. It opened.

"Master Bryden, sir, it's your breakfast tray." I entered slowly. The room smelled of bay rum and whiskey. Sun streamed through wide-open windows, and on the balcony, in a large chair, sat Master Bryden. He didn't move when I approached.

His long black hair had been cut short. I lowered the tray to a nearby table.

"Sir?"

"Who are you?" His voice sounded distant.

"Finsloe, sir. I'm sorry to have intruded. I've brought your breakfast."

"Finsloe?"

His deep voice penetrated my nerves.

My voice quavered. "I'm to be your valet."

"I'll not be here long enough to need a valet." His head drooped. "Some things cannot be replaced."

"Of course, sir."

He leaned forward and struggled to stand. I went to him.

"I'm fine." He lifted himself painfully from the chair. "Is there coffee?"

"Yes, sir." I went to the tray. "And tea, toast, eggs, sausages, pastries—"

"Just black coffee, please."

I poured a cup and brought it to him. Until then, I'd not looked at him, and when he took the cup from me, I stared into his eyes.

He took the cup from me and brought it to his lips. "What is it?"

"Nothing, sir. Can I run a bath for you, sir?"

"Why can't I remember you, Finsloe?" He returned back to the balcony and stared straight ahead.

"I don't know, sir." My heart cracked. In an attempt to stanch my heartache I looked around and gathered his scattered clothes.

"You must forgive my lack of memory; I've been tormented with so many things as of late that I barely remember these rooms." He choked over the last word.

I piled his clothes in the basket left in the corner by the door. "It doesn't matter."

"It does matter!" He came away from the balcony. "I don't understand..."

I went to him and took his cup to refill. "Have a small bite, and I will run a bath. There's indoor plumbing now; no need to call the water man to fill and heat the tub."

"How miraculous." He looked around him. "The house has changed, and yet everything is the same."

I moved a small table beside the chair he'd sat in and placed the tray on it. When I turned, he stood close to me. "Poached eggs and toast, then a bath," I stammered.

Bryden glanced down at the eggs. "Will you stay awhile? I cannot bear being alone with my thoughts this morning." He sat down. "I will eat, but please call me Bryden. I never could abide being called 'Master'; my former valet always called me..."

"What was his name?"

"Jonathan."

"What happened to Jonathan?" I realized I'd overstepped my place. "I didn't mean to—"

He lifted his hands to his face. "I'd always prided myself at being an expert seaman. My hands are a testament to my skill."

"Sir...Bryden, please, you don't have to speak of it."

"Each year," he continued as though I hadn't spoken, "my hands grew stronger, until I could steer any vessel, guide any sail and hold any rope, but that day I couldn't hold on; the wind and the sea proved stronger." His voice trembled. "Jonathan was tossed from the boat." Bryden looked wild eyed. "I couldn't save him. I wanted to, I tried to, but couldn't. He slipped through my fingers." He wiped a hand across his face and took a deep breath. "It's been a year since I lost him. I loved him, you see. I loved him terribly." A tear ran down his cheek. "You must think I'm a fool."

"No, I think you're exhausted and hungry. I don't think you're a fool. You are brave to have loved as you pleased."

"Brave?" Bryden grabbed the napkin I'd placed on the table and swiped at his eyes. "I don't know about that."

But I did know. I'd wanted to know the love Bryden felt for Jonathan, waited for someone to name it and prove it possible.

I put a hand on his shoulder. "Eat and I will stay with you awhile."

Bryden cut into a poached egg, and lifted the fork to his mouth. "The eggs are perfect." He stared at the egg a moment and then took the bite and chewed thoughtfully.

A smear of yolk glistened on his bottom lip and I crouched beside him, then took the napkin and pressed it to his mouth. The linen slipped below my thumb, and my finger slid against the plump skin of his lips. Our eyes met.

"I remember you," he whispered.

Heat burned my cheeks and I dropped the napkin and stood. "Shall I prepare a bath?"

Bryden nodded, but his eyes bore into me and he stared after me as I left the room.

While I filled the tub, wanton memories teased my mind: his

sensuous mouth, the strong line of his chin and the curve of his shoulders. I wanted him terribly.

"If you're ready, sir?" I called, but needn't have, because he stood in the bathroom doorway.

Bryden removed his robe. When it slid to the floor, I went to retrieve it.

"Leave it." Bryden undid the knot of his waistband, and his pajama bottoms fell to his ankles. Naked, he revealed a geography not only of muscle, and beauty, but of scars, bruises and exhaustion. His cock rested against his balls beneath a thatch of dark hair. It twitched under my gaze.

"You're wounded."

Bryden looked down. "It's nothing." He approached the tub. "I'll heal." He lifted one thickly muscled leg and then the other and cautiously lowered himself into the steamy water. Pain clouded his face.

"Should I fetch a doctor?"

"No." He forced a smile. "You should sit beside me."

I positioned a cushioned stool near the tub, and sat.

Bryden closed his eyes and sighed. "I've missed a bath."

"Where have you been that you did not have a bath?"

"At sea. We traveled for months at a time, just the two of us. We bathed in the ocean."

"You drifted."

"For as long as we could," he replied, quietly.

"May I ask you something?"

"Anything." He opened one eye. "What is it?"

"There's been talk."

He closed his eye. "There's always talk."

"They say there were mysterious circumstances."

Bryden sat up abruptly. Water splashed over the edge of the tub. Fire burned in his eyes. "The men who challenged me last night mentioned such talk. You should seek them out and see what they believe now."

"I meant only to alert you of things being said." I gathered a towel and mopped the floor, as Bryden settled back into the tub.

I took the large sponge floating in the water and drenched it. "Let me help."

His eyes appraised me. "Do you believe such talk?"

I shook my head. "Not a word."

He leaned forward, and I squeezed the sponge so warm water ran down his back.

He groaned appreciatively. "Thank you."

"How long will you stay?" I moved the sponge along his shoulders, careful of his wounds.

"Not long."

"Where will you go?"

"I've no idea."

I dropped the sponge and sat back on the stool.

"What is it?"

"I have to go." I stood and left the bathroom.

"Finsloe?"

I made it to the bedroom door before he caught me; when I opened the door he grabbed my arm.

"Listen to me!"

"I can't."

He let my arm go, but shut the door. "Years ago, the night before I was sent away, I crept upstairs to the garret."

"Please, I can't bear it when you'll leave...or drift away."

He moved against me. "I couldn't leave without touching you one last time. I was a coward to have done it the way I did."

"What do you mean, *sent away*? You left for university."

He shook his head violently. "I was sent away because my

parents suspected an imperfection in their perfect son."

"All this time you loved someone, while I hid in closets, pantries and darkness longing for what you had with Jonathan." I exhaled loudly when he put his arms around me.

"I wouldn't have been brave enough to find it if you hadn't loved me first." He tightened his grip. "I wanted you until I couldn't want you anymore. Each day I wandered was another day I wanted to come home. But when I met Jonathan and he looked at me the way you did, the world opened up again." He rested his chin on my shoulder. "I didn't expect to find you here with the same look in your eyes."

"I'm happy you found love."

He cast his eyes downward. "Found and lost it."

I kissed him because words ceased to have meaning, and we sought relief from sorrow in each other's lips.

Bryden pulled away. "We aren't flawed, Finsloe." Dazed, I nodded as he undid my tie. "You were always so loyal." His fingers undid the buttons of my vest. "I owe you so very much." He tugged my shirt from my trousers and tore it open. "Let me make it up to you."

I shook beneath his touch. "You owe me nothing."

He loosened my belt. "Come to my bed."

Bryden continued to undress me as we walked, pausing to kiss my chin, my neck, my face. I begged him to never stop. I wanted time to stand still because, behind my frenzied pleasure, I wondered if I could bear it when he left again.

By the time we tumbled onto the bed, I'd been stripped naked and our bodies melded together. I searched him as an explorer who has unearthed a new map. Each muscle, ridge and curve led to further sumptuous pleasure.

I moaned when his mouth found my nipples; he rolled one between his fingers while his mouth sucked on the other. When his teeth grazed the tender skin, I yelped, and he responded by sucking harder until I dug my fingers into his back. He grunted and removed his mouth.

"Last time I used my hands." Bryden's hand slid along the side of my thigh. "But I think my mouth would be better this time." He moved his hand across my leg and took my hard cock in it. "Just like I remember."

I'd wanked to the thought of Bryden's mouth on my cock many times. Now, as he kissed his way down my stomach, I realized the fantasy paled next to the reality.

"I remember how hard you were." His eyes flashed with pleasure.

I turned my head, embarrassed by his enjoyment of my cock.

"Why do you blush?" He stroked my cock. "Do you remember this?"

I nodded into the pillow, still unable to face him.

He stroked faster. "I wanted you so badly. For months I pleasured myself thinking about you."

"You did?"

He grinned up at me. "So many times." His mouth opened before he lowered it to the tip of my cock. His tongue played with my foreskin.

I shuddered and watched as he urged pearly droplets of fluid from the tip.

He slurped hungrily, then took the head into his mouth.

I groaned and grasped at the pillows.

His mouth slid down along my shaft.

"Bryden!" My balls ached and tightened against my cock. Bryden tugged on them until I cried out for him to stop.

He released them and came off my cock. His mouth was shiny with spit, and he licked his lips. "You taste," he rolled his eyes as if trying to find the word, "incredible."

I laughed aloud.

He grinned. "It's true, and I want more of you." He spit down on his cock. I felt the tip tease my ass. Nerves fired through my body, my gut churning. I'd never been taken by a man before, and fearful shame made me inch away.

Bryden placed a hand on my belly. "Do you want me to stop?" He slid a finger between his lips, then lowered it to my ass. His spit-slick digit circled my hole.

"Put it inside." I begged.

Slowly, he worked past my fear, and I accepted his finger. His interior exploration made me dizzy. My breath came short and fast as he went deeper, while his free hand found and stroked my cock.

My legs began to shake. "Use your cock," I gasped.

Carefully he removed his finger and lifted my legs, so that one rested on each shoulder.

The absence of his finger made me twinge with expectancy. I wanted to be full of him. I'd waited long enough.

He moved in and urged the head of his cock inside. "If it hurts…"

I shook my head.

He went farther.

I heard him moan, but I'd lost myself in his thrust. Sparks erupted behind my eyes. I scooted toward his cock and welcomed him deeper inside.

"Fuck!" he cried out as his cock buried itself in my ass. I clenched, not wanting to let him go. We stayed like this a blissful minute. My insides savored his intrusion.

When he moved, I bit my lip.

"I'm going to fuck you now," he grunted.

"I want you to." I looked at him and saw pleasure on his face.

Slowly, then fast and slow again, he filled me with his cock. Each time sent me farther over the edge. I stroked my cock and bucked my hips against him, feeling intensified bliss with each plunge of his prick. He must have realized that the depth of his fuck was going to make me come because he drove deeper and faster.

Unintelligible words came from my mouth as my body gave itself to the wave of joyous release. I surrendered as rope after rope of my seed splashed up across his gut then fell back onto my chest.

Seconds later, I watched Bryden's cock emerge, thick and swollen.

I watched, fascinated by his beauty and intensity, as he stroked himself. His body convulsed with the ferocity of one who had long neglected his needs. The come came hard and fast from his cock. The muscles twitched beneath the skin on his belly and chest, veins standing in stark relief along his arms.

The warmth of his pearly rain soaked my skin and ran along my sides. He shook his cock until the last drop fell. His moans quieted and his body stilled.

Spent, he fell beside me and urged my arms around him.

"You're perfect," he whispered.

I held him tight. "How long will you stay?"

He sighed. "Not long."

My heart ached. "Where will you go?"

"Don't know." He looked up. "But wherever it is, I hope you'll come with me."

# BOOTING

## Salome Wilde

No one would ever call my former employer, Lord Tithenham, dull witted, though dull witted he was, along with the whole born-to-wealth lot of them at Tithenham Court—and most anywhere you find titled gentry these days. Like to like, I always say, and that's how they've done on this island for as long as anyone can remember. Those below do all the work, and those above feel they've earned their leisure through God-given grace. Without their staff, they'd be lost, just sitting around in the clothes last put on them until they starved to death. You'll note I no longer include myself among the Tithenham staff. They once counted me in their tidy, obedient number, but no longer. Though I'm still in service elsewhere and do as I'm told, I'm not like the others, nor ever will be.

If no one would call Tithenham dull, no one at Tithenham Court would ever have called me smart. More fools they, say I. They didn't much even call me Davie, though that is my name. I was "boot lad" or simply "Hey, boy," though I was and am sharp as a blade and then some. For proof, take for a starter that I'm writing this and you're reading it. I can write and you can read, and though I can't rightly say whether reading this makes you sharp or dull, you must be a queer sod to want to read the details of my sordid tale—and for that, I salute you.

When I first earned the post of boot boy, I was told I should be grateful. And, as it suited me better than sweeping floors or mucking stalls in the village, I was indeed; in truth, it provided a break from harder work. And before you misunderstand, I don't mean that stable or inn work was harder than cleaning shit off boots and polishing them until they shine like a dishonest grin. No, it's just that the kind of side work I've always found most profitable is best done in the manors of the well-to-do. And, in the end, it was my position at Tithenham Court that led to the life I have now. As I've said, I'm still in service, but with benefits unknown and undreamt of by most household staff, whatever their rank.

What I've come to call "side work" is likely what makes this story of sufficient interest that these pages are in anyone's hands but my own right now. In the case of life at Tithenham (which you've no doubt by now realized is not the real name of my former place of residence and employment, nor are any other names herein, as I've no more desire to wind up in prison for my adventures than you have for reading about them), I found myself favored by young Lord Tithenham, also known as Reggie. He'd returned from college to begin a country squire's life, someday to inherit both land and title. By agreeing to marry some unsavory second cousin and thus solidify the future of the Tithenham legacy, he'd made both a wise and disappointing decision. In me, he found a sympathetic ear. And then he found more. Even after he claimed his bride, he continued to claim me as well—and none too gently—whenever opportunity presented itself. I praised his prick, deferred to his whims and earned no little coin and privilege for it. As I'm older than I look, and look quite good for a gap-toothed child of low birth, life under Reggie (as it were) seemed to promise all I could desire.

One fine evening off, my luck brought me an extra opportunity to boot. I was sitting in the corner of the Three Lambs, sipping beer with a few locals, listening to tales of farmer's daughters and petty theft, and enjoying a break from quibbling scullery maids and ignorant under-cooks for a change. Had they—and especially Richfield, that nosy and jaundiced butler—known where I was or with whom I was consorting, I'd have been let go on the spot. But my dear benefactor Reggie had seen to it that all knew I was generously visiting a sick aunt on my evenings off, so all was well.

In fact, all was better than well when I chanced to see two men enter the inn, cloaks close around their shoulders, though the weather was clement. They asked spotty old Mrs. Dewberry for a room for the night and waited in the main hall while she fixed them a meal. I looked them over quite unseen, and when they took their food and drink to one of the small upstairs rooms, I got the good Mrs. D. to tell me all.

The two claimed to be brothers, young men on a trip across country. Sadly, one of their horses had come down lame. They'd put the other up and were spending the night to start afresh in the morning with whatever new animal they could procure. Mrs. D. wasn't the suspicious type, especially when she was well paid, but I was. And I was certain these fellows were neither brothers nor travelers.

I'd seen them touch, for one, the calm, taller man putting his arm around the smaller one's shoulders to remove his cloak and later dab at a splash of wine on his shirt. And when he smiled down at his nervous companion, murmuring, "Let's go,

Percy" or "Phillip" or something of the like, I knew there was a ruse afoot. More was revealed as they mounted the stairs. If I knew anything from my time at Tithenham, it was the make of a boot. Disguise themselves as they might, I knew the style and cost of the boots they wore. The two were master and servant; I'd have sworn my prick on it. Though they were unlike young Lord Reggie and I—for the master here was the smaller man and the servant the taller and obvious leader of their adventure—they were indulging in the same basic exchange. Everything is given away if you're observant enough, and I saw all. And I saw even more than all when, an hour later, I burst into their room, stuttering, "I'm so terribly sorry," and "I had no idea..."

"Get the hell out!" the tall man barked, turning to face the door while keeping a kneeling position on the sagging bed, where he'd been fucking young Phillip or Percy.

Percy or Phillip whined pitifully and buried his face in the worn bed linen, but I couldn't truly tell whether it was my discovery or the break in the arse-pounding that brought forth the not-unfamiliar sound. (I'd happily made such mewls myself on more than a few occasions, truth be told.)

"Is the lad all right?" I asked with mock earnestness, closing the door behind me. "Shall I fetch a doctor?"

The man hastily withdrew from his target and hopped off the bed. He cut his eyes at me in a most rousing manner as he approached. His slender body and perfect posture—clearly that of a servant, a second footman if I guessed correctly—was handsome enough, and his cock was wet and still stiff with pride.

"Don't make me force you to get out, you little rat," he said through gritted teeth. The poor fool on the bed let out a whimper of dismay, entertainingly keeping his bottom up and face down. His dangling sac offered a small, pink eyeful, behind which, it seemed, Little Percy or Phillip remained hidden from my appraising gaze.

"Quiet now, Pip," said the servant in charge, still giving me the eye. "I'll manage this."

"Oh yes, Pip," I echoed with a smirk, folding my arms as I leaned against the door. "Never you fear." Though I was slight, I wasn't going to back down from this easy catch.

"Shut it, you," the fellow before me snapped, and young master Pip was instantly silent. Turning his head and taking a step back, he reached to push the moronic fellow's bottom down. He cooed reassurances, making clear that his demand for silence was of me. Then he returned, continuing to fail to intimidate me.

We both knew that a fight was exactly what he couldn't afford. Mrs. Dewberry and her plentiful patrons downstairs would be sure to hear a commotion and come running. The Mrs. would want to be sure her furniture and windows weren't broken, and the blokes would come for a gander and maybe even a wager. Yes, the servant would have to use whatever wits he could summon to dispatch me without a fuss.

To remind him, I said with kindly tone, "Come now, that's no way to talk. It's not my fault I stumbled into the wrong room, is it? How could I know what you two young *brothers* might be up to?" I widened my grin, unable to temper my enjoyment.

"You little prick," my opponent sneered, his slack cock bobbing as he swept his hair from his face with an angry flourish.

"Actually, it's rather large, I've been told," I replied, gripping and shaking it beneath my loose, tattered trousers. "Maybe I should take a turn with the gentleman there, if—"

The bloke's fist shot out, and I dodged, just in time. The blow landed with a bang into the door and he swore, while Pip gave a muffled squawk from beneath the blankets, where he'd since wrapped himself.

I shook my head. "One more of those and you'll be sorry," I warned as my foe rubbed his knuckles. I couldn't tell whether he actually felt some affection for the poor little master or if he was just protecting his own pretty arse. I was leaning toward the latter.

"All right," he said with a sigh. "How much do you want?"

Now we were getting somewhere. I knew he wasn't as foolish as he was acting. But he was wrong to have tried to bust my face, and I'd make him sorry for it. "Oh dear," I tutted, "are you trying to buy me off? An honest lad like me? Why, I couldn't take money for having seen what I did; it wouldn't be right."

Pip stopped shuddering and poked his inbred weasel's face from the blankets. I smiled broadly at him, showing my impressive mouthful of crooked teeth. He winced. I knew now he wasn't quite as young as I'd hoped, clearly of age. That was a disappointment. It'd take my price down some, but there was still profit to be made. What they were up to was scandalous, not to mention criminal, and the servant would lose his position at the very least if I told. If the footman was as smart as I was, of course, he'd lay it all on the pitiful Pip and take some cash for his troubles. But then he'd have to get away quick, and might never find a position as good as he had, assuming he liked what he did as much as I.

"You won't tell anyone, then," Pip at last found the courage to pipe, his tone somewhere between a plea and a command.

The servant raised an eyebrow. He was embarrassed by Pip's outburst, I could tell, and sizing me up at the same time. I doubted he'd size correctly, but I enjoyed having him look me over. I followed suit. Steady brown eyes, he had, and a nice wide mouth. I could see why the weakling Pip was smitten. I turned my gaze back to the bed. "Well now, I didn't say I wouldn't tell..." I told him, letting my words trail off to make clear their meaning to even the dullest of gentry.

My adversary cleared his throat. "Suppose we let the young gentleman on the bed take his leave so we can discuss the matter further, Mister...?"

"Davie," I answered with a wink. "Just Davie."

"And I'm James," he replied with a generous grin, and headed for the chair where Pip's costume lay. He took up the garments and held them out to Pip, who reached a timid arm to snatch them. "Come along now," James admonished. It seemed the young gent was afraid to expose himself.

"Don't be frightened, young sir," I added, enthusiastically. "I've already seen your best bits."

James bit his lip to keep from laughing, and I had to do the same. Though I needed to keep the upper hand, James was one of my kind. With another clearing of his throat, he reasserted his outrage in my direction, obviously for Pip's benefit, demanding I turn my "bleedin' back" while he helped the young master to dress and depart.

I agreed humbly and faced the wall, warning, "No tricks, now," with relish.

The grumbling sounds of the indignant Pip as he hastily clothed himself in his rough ware were almost as entertaining as the sight of his scrawny pale flesh being stuffed into it. Neither man seemed to notice that I'd turned to peek once or twice, nor that my eyes were more on James than Pip.

At last, the servant rushed his master to the door, murmuring to him about finding his way to the stables to retrieve their horse and head back home. Brave Pip could at least ride, it seemed, but the child-man still protested under his breath. I found it almost sweet that he feared James might not be able to find his way home. Absurd, yes, but sweet.

Still naked as the day he was born but delightfully grown, James shut the door behind young Pip to find me lounging on the bed, back propped by pillows and hands behind my head. "So, Jimmy," I said, "shall we negotiate?"

"That's James," he replied, mounting the bed and roughly pushing my legs apart to climb between them.

"Nice opening bid," I answered.

He chuckled low as he hovered over me, ably unfastening with one hand the rope that tied my pants. "I hope I can offer enough to get you to hold that wicked little tongue of yours, boy."

"Davie," I said.

"Davie." He shoved his hand inside to give my prick a good tug, while I bucked into his grip. "You work here?"

I was incensed. "'Course not. I'm in service up at Tithenham. Just happened to spot you while I was having a pint on my evening off."

He nodded, and I could see his mind working. "Boot boy, I'll wager."

"And what's it to you, footman?"

"Second footman," he answered, jerking me again.

I sneered, but within a few strokes I was losing my desire to argue. I tipped my head back and closed my eyes, practically humming for more. Though I'd had my share of willing gals, there was nothing like the grip of a man who knew what he was about. I felt his lips at my throat next and then his tongue. I was rocking into his fist with a good, steady rhythm when he suddenly stopped. I opened my eyes to find him moving back to take my pants down. I shrugged. Why not? It wouldn't alter my price, but it was a welcome distraction and a change from the local boys and pasty Master Reggie, that was sure. Once they were off, I sat up and pulled my shirt over my head. I wasn't exactly clean, but then neither was he. I tossed him my shirt and nodded toward his dick. "Wipe that arse's arse off your cock," I ordered.

He laughed and rose. "He may be an arse, but I had him, and you, little wretch, spoiled my plans." He poured water from the pitcher onto a cloth and stroked his shaft while I took in his meaning. "Better now?" he asked, spreading his arms to show off his clean, hard tackle.

I nodded and welcomed him back into my arms. I liked the weight of him: not too heavy, not too light. And when he kissed me and we ground our bodies together, I liked him even more. There was roughness to his mouth and force in his tongue that matched mine well. And we made sweet, low sounds together, hardness to hardness. It was only when he pulled away again, shifting to reach beneath my knees and pull them back, that I caught my breath and came to my senses. "Hey," I said, scooting back against the headboard, "I'm not your young master, you know."

He laughed, eyes soft with need, as mine must have been. "You certainly aren't. You're a street brat with a touch of luck is what you are. Bet you haven't washed in a week."

"Two days," I spat back, feeling childish. I'd catch hell, after all, if Cook found me stinking up her kitchen when I came to the table. "And I've more than luck or you wouldn't be kissing me like that, now would you?" I ran my tongue over my lips, tasting James on them.

He shook his head, still smiling widely. "All right, then. Say you've got something. Say I like the way you talk. Well, it's time to see if there's more I like." He grabbed my ankles and pulled me back down.

I pressed against his chest as he laid his body on mine again.

"Wait now," I demanded, and rolled out from under him and onto my feet beside the bed.

"Damn but you're quick." He rose, too, and stalked me back to the wall before kissing me hard as he dug his hands into my rump to pull us together.

I moaned, though I didn't mean to, and then I nipped his tongue. He grabbed my face and narrowed his eyes. "Just what game are we playing here, Davie?" His breath was hot and so was his cock, pressing hard into my belly.

I couldn't break away, but then, I didn't really want to. "That's what I want to know," I mumbled.

He released my chin and shrugged. "Seems to me we're just getting to know each other. What's it seem like to you?"

"Like you're trying to take advantage of the situation," I answered, more confidently.

He shrugged. "And if I am?"

I didn't have an answer for that. And though I couldn't figure how I'd gone from having all the control to giving it up to some second footman I'd only met minutes ago, I wanted to give it. The rest we'd figure out later. "There's oil in the lamp," I offered.

James laughed heartily and lifted me up, then hoisted me over his shoulder. "You forget, I came prepared."

I laughed a feeble protest at being hauled about like dirty laundry. James walked me the two steps back to the bed and, with a grunt, tossed me down and fell with passion upon me. We writhed, mouth to mouth and cock to cock, with renewed fervor, all thoughts beyond the moment's selfish pleasure banished. But I'd be missed downstairs if I took too long, so, when he rose up again, I spread my legs wide and lifted my knees for him. "Time to fetch that *preparation*," I said, with as much charm as I could from such a position, and then he laughed and fetched.

There was something beautiful about the way he slathered himself, polishing the pole, while I watched. And he liked me watching, I could tell. But soon the show was over and he poured a bit more from a little bottle onto his fingers and fed two into me, slow and steady. I smelled something flowery, lavender maybe, and smiled at the idea of young Pip needing perfume for his hole. "Nice," I said as he slicked me good and got me going. I hadn't experienced this kind of thing much; Reggie hadn't a lot to him, and he might oil himself up, but never me.

James dug deeper and pumped his fingers. I gasped and clenched my jaw at the rightness of it. He hit the spot perfect and just kept hitting it. I arched into his hand and suddenly felt him take hold of my stick. It was achy-sweet the way he milked me while he fingered me, but before long I couldn't take it. "I'll spill!" I spat, wanting it bad, but wanting the fuck even more.

"Easy now, Davie," he said, slipping his fingers out and letting go of my cock.

I moaned at the loss, then stilled, not wanting to sound like whiny-boy Pip. And when James drew my legs around his waist as he came on to me, I thrilled that I wasn't being turned onto all fours. Not that I didn't enjoy it slapping rough, but right now I wanted to feel James enjoying it as much as I did. He clamped his mouth over mine before I could tell him so and spoil the moment, and then guided himself in.

He was so stiff, just the way you need to be to get it in and make it right for both parties concerned. Thoughts came of half-hard Reggie, with all of his arrogance and guilt, fucking me more to punish his family than because he fancied me. Some punishment that! Such thoughts—along with any others—flew from my mind as James neatly forced the bulb in past the muscles I was working to relax. He groaned into my mouth, and I, in turn, ate it up.

"Yes," he hissed, "good and tight."

I felt proud and dizzy, throbbing as he stretched me wide and filled me up. "Fuck," I spat as he hilted and just held it there. He drew his teeth along my jaw as I clutched his hips with my knees, ankles locked around his back. His hands were planted on either side of my head and he reared up with a grin, still deep inside me, unmoving. I looked into his heavy-lidded eyes, thick black hair hanging over them. I felt cool air hit my cock, and I shivered.

"Right," he said, like a servant getting down to work, which, I suppose, he was. His smile widened, though I myself couldn't manage one.

I was holding my breath, I realized, and when I drew in another he began to fuck me, good and hard. We groaned and grunted together, soon making it hard to tell whose sounds were whose. He pounded deep, his balls slapping my arse with each stroke, while I hung on for the ride. Whether he was leaning in to press against my shaft as he went or just finding an angle he liked, I wasn't sure, but between that and the way my hips were tipped, I was rising as fast as he.

Soon, I was biting back my finish with all my strength while he was plowing on, taking what he needed the way he needed it. He huffed and growled, and I fought to keep my eyes open to enjoy the sight of him as he dripped sweat down upon me. I unclenched one hand from around his shoulder and threaded my fingers through the dark, moist hair on his chest, then rubbed across a small, hard nipple. He moaned at this and helped me keep my release at bay by leaning up and off my cock so I could pinch and roll first one then the other stiff nub. Though he was driving me on with ferocious power, I relished that I was giving him pleasure with not only my tight, willing hole but my able fingers, too.

It couldn't last forever, of course, and all at once he threw his body fully over mine. Grinding hard while I held him with arms and legs both, he made a harsh, choking sound—no doubt the training of having to do it on the quiet so often—and, keeping his pace without stopping, I gritted my teeth and spent myself, hurdling over the edge with such sharpness that I only knew he'd found his release when he slowed and shuddered through every inch of his body.

All was silent save our panting. I untwined myself and James rolled off, both of us edging over to give enough room to lie on our backs, side by side, and to catch our breaths. I brushed hair from my eyes and wiped the blanket across my sticky belly.

"A bit of a mess, I see," James quipped, still puffing a bit.

"Inside and out," I hoarsely replied. I coughed. "I need a drink."

James sat up and squeezed his cock dry, then reached under to scratch. "Wash and a smoke for me."

I nodded and made the effort to rise. I was light-headed and flopped back down with a sigh.

From my supine position, I watched James stand and stretch and then head for the pitcher. He splashed his face, his neck and his armpits, followed by his now-slack cock and loose-hanging balls.

"That felt damned good," I offered, just enjoying the sight of him.

He pivoted and pointed a finger. "But it didn't pay," he said, quickly back to business.

"It'd better pay me," I said, forcing myself up on my elbows. If he was going to talk sharp then so was I.

He snorted as he headed toward his clothes that lay in a heap on the chair by the door. "Little schemer, you."

I smiled as my heart raced. "And you as well."

Instead of dressing, he dug into his coat pocket and pulled

out a cigarette and a match. He returned to the bed and sat beside me before lighting up.

"Tell you what," he said, taking a deep drag and exhaling through his nose. "I've got an idea that'll give us both what we deserve."

I was wary, knowing I couldn't trust the handsome James any more than anyone else in this life, but as I stared at the quirk of his pretty red mouth, I found myself nodding him on.

"You know Clarington Hall, I suppose," he began.

I nodded again. Who didn't know Clarington Hall? The earl's estate was more than twice the size of Tithenham.

"That's where I'm in service," he said proudly.

"And?" I prodded, trying my hardest to sound unimpressed, though it was a fool's game; I was all ears and he knew it.

James smiled and stroked my hair with his free hand. "Well, little Davie the boot boy, it just so happens that the staff is about to have a vacancy for your very position."

"About to have?"

"Seems young Toby's been stealing the parlor maids' underthings, you see, and if Evans—our old sot of a butler— finds out, he won't be having it, I can tell you."

I caught James's hand and took a slow drag off his cigarette. He watched me. "I see," I said, blowing smoke. And I did.

James slipped an arm around my shoulder. "How lucky my trustworthy cousin Davie just happens to be a devoted little boot boy himself," he mused happily.

"Lucky indeed," said I, flashing a grin. Already I was packing my things and on the way to Clarington in my mind.

"Oh, the trouble we'll cause, Davie," he added with a wink, flicking ash onto the threadbare rug. "The fun we'll find."

And so indeed we have.

# SEDUCING
# THE FOOTMAN

## Brent Archer

Trenton Pennington walked across the small lodge to wind up the gramophone. His Uncle Thomas had brought the new machine back with him from a trip to America last year. None of the other estates in his section of Somerset had one, which certainly made Trenton a man in demand with the local ladies. Sadly for them, however, he wasn't interested in their fawning and prattling.

He replaced the round disc with a new record, grasped the handle and wound up the machine. With gentle ease, he positioned the needle on the arm at the edge of the disc, a lively polka instantly filling the room. Satisfied the music was adequate, he went to the small cabinet by a curtained window and took out two crystal-stemmed glasses. A bottle of red wine waited on the countertop.

He poured the dark liquid into the glasses and turned back to the settee across the room. The young man sitting there smiled a cheeky grin, his arms spread along the back of the sofa. Desire stirred in Trenton's midsection as a smile played across his own lips. They had the entire afternoon, after all, and Trenton wasn't going to let the young footman out of the lodge until they were both satisfied.

The footman shifted on the settee as Trenton approached, pulling off his black bow tie and opening the top button of his pressed white shirt. "Why did you ask me here, sir? Won't Lady Pennington miss me?"

"My mother is in London for the next fortnight. Sister Emily is away at Callam Hall and my brother William seems to be chasing the new maid at the moment while his wife is away with Mama." He sat next to the young man and offered him the wine.

"That is very nice of you, sir."

Trenton raised his glass. "To new acquaintances."

"To your health, sir."

"Please, there's no need to be formal while we're out here alone. Call me Trent."

The young man looked down at his glass and then into his master's eyes. "Thank you, sir...uh, I mean Trent."

They drank, and then Trenton swirled the wine in his glass and held it up to the sunlight that poured through the window. "This is a corking little vintage. Ramsey Killington brought it back from Turkey last year when he went on his grand tour. Still haven't decided where to go for mine. A man of twenty-three should have gone already, but I can't decide whether to go to Cairo or Saint Petersburg."

"It's not my place to say, sir."

"Trent."

"Sorry. Trent."

Trenton smiled. "Don't be silly. I'm interested in your opinion. Have you traveled before?"

"No, sir, I haven't left the estate on any real adventure, though I dream of going to Amsterdam some day."

He knew, of course, that the footman hadn't traveled before, but now his interest was piqued. "Why Amsterdam?"

"All the water. I'm fascinated with canals and waterways."

Trenton tapped his chin. "Perhaps one day I could find an excuse to take you abroad with me."

The young man's green eyes widened. "Thank you, sir. I'd like that indeed."

"Trent."

"Sorry. Trent."

Trenton set his glass down on the small table next to the sofa and edged in closer. "Dash it all, I'm so rude. I didn't ask what you'd prefer to be called."

The young man met his gaze. "I'm John. John Cable."

"How long have you worked on the estate, John?"

He set his glass down next to Trenton's. "I've lived on the estate all my life. My mum is one of the servants to her ladyship. I came into your employ after I finished with my schooling."

"So you're eighteen?"

He frowned. "Twenty. Mum started me late because I was ill for a couple years early on."

Trenton took his glass and sat back, sipping at the wine. John hadn't moved his arm off the back of the settee, and Trenton reveled in the warmth emanating from it. "So tell me, has any lady caught your attention?"

He smirked. "No, Trent, no *ladies* have stirred my interest."

*Promising.* Trenton took another sip of wine.

John unbuttoned the top two buttons of his shirt. "What of you? Why are you not engaged or married yet, like your brother?"

Trenton rolled his eyes. "Father wants me to marry Janet

Meikle from Scotland. Can you imagine? That rough brogue filling the dining room when the lords and ladies dine with us?"

John moved his arm from behind Trenton and unbuttoned the cuffs at his wrists. "But what do *you* want?"

He looked deeply into John's eyes. A sexy smile spread across his face as the footman's finger trailed down his master's sleeve. This was not quite as planned. Trenton was supposed to seduce the hot young servant. *Who's the quarry and who's the hawk?* Trenton squirmed in his seat, trying to keep his composure as his desire stirred further. He didn't want to fall under John's control, as he was accustomed to calling the shots. "I don't know what I want. I do know I don't want *her*."

John laughed. "Seems an easy one to me then. Tell your father you're not going to marry her."

Trenton's eyes widened. "Telling my father no is like telling King Edward you'd rather not come to Court—it just isn't done."

John sat back. "I've heard that Scotland is lovely this time of year."

Trenton arched his eyebrow. "And where did you hear that?"

"A handsome young Scot told me at school. Actually, he taught me *many* things that year."

Trenton leaned toward him. "Such as?"

"Such as this." John reached out his hands to grasp Trenton's hair and crushed their lips together like a pirate plundering a merchant ship.

Trenton tried to push away, grabbing John's wrists, but quickly dropped his hands and yielded to the desire the young man awakened in him. His kiss was a flame stoking the fire of his lust.

John broke the kiss, and Trenton locked eyes with the seductive man yet again. "This is what you want, isn't it?"

Trenton could barely manage a whisper. "Yes."

John stood and held out his hand. "Let's go upstairs." John led him into the small entryway and up the stone steps to the second floor. Three bedroom doors greeted them.

Trenton took the lead and pulled John into the first one. He closed the door and turned just in time to receive another scorching kiss. Any thoughts of dominance faded as John pulled at his clothes. Trousers, garters, shirt, stockings, tie. All fell to the floor as he was quickly stripped to his undergarments.

John pushed him onto the bed and stood before him. He turned away and bent over to pick up Trenton's clothes, pushing out his round ass in his neatly pressed black pants. He looked over his shoulder at Trenton. "Is this to your liking, sir?"

Trenton's throat went dry, nerves suddenly surfacing as his underling seduced him. He'd never been so aroused in his entire life.

"Yes," he gasped.

John rose and placed the clothes onto the dresser next to the bed. He faced Trenton and carefully removed and folded his own attire. Each revelation of perfect pale flesh left his master panting, his cock swelling and pushing against his undershorts. The thrill of anticipation threatened to drive him mad as the footman stayed just out of reach on the pretext of being neat.

Finally, the seductive servant stood before the bed naked with his hands on his hips. Trenton drank in his beautiful body. His clean-shaven face was still boyish, framed in curly dark hair. Green eyes stalked him as they looked across a button nose, his pouty lips forming into a grin. His torso was devoid of hair with the exception of two dark wisps around his nipples and a thatch under each arm. A thin line of hair led from his navel to a patch of dense swirling curls framing a thick manhood and heavy balls. His legs were covered in hair, leading down to sturdy feet.

Trenton reclined on the bed and spread his legs. "You're very much to my liking."

John padded forward with stealth, like the moves of a lion about to pounce. "Do you know what you want?" His eyes were mesmerizing. Trenton's gaze locked onto those green eyes. Yes. In this moment of seduction, clarity dawned bright and blazing. He knew what he wanted. "You."

"Then you shall have me." John leapt onto the bed, pinning Trenton's arms above his head with one hand and tearing at the remaining fabric covering his body with the other. "You'll get exactly what you want."

John's mouth ravaged Trenton's lips before moving down to his neck. The man beneath gasped, trying to free his hands as his body was lost in a wave of passion. His fingers longed to touch John's flesh, but were denied, increasing his desire all the more. John continued his journey, exploring every peak and valley of the nobleman's form. His tongue darted into the thick patch of blond hair under Trenton's arms, the master thrashing from side to side as class distinction and reason fell away; only blinding lust remained.

Trenton's cock strained as each lick and nip at his flesh sent fire through his body. As John sucked on a nipple, he gasped. "Good lord, what are you doing to me?"

John released the nub from between his lips. "Pleasuring you like a Scot without the burden of marriage." He resumed his ravaging.

Trenton, still pinned to the bed, was helpless to resist—though resistance was the last thing on his mind. He rode the waves of sensations, many new to him, as his pleasure and desire reached a fevered crescendo, like the chords of the polka still playing in the room below. John's chest rubbed against Trenton's hardness as he worked his nipple and then spread kisses across his belly.

A tingling built up in Trenton's tightened balls, his orgasm imminent. He thrashed, bucking his hips against John's chest. John finally released his arms, grabbing Trenton's shoulders as he pulled him up into a kiss. John's thickness ground against Trenton's aching cock, and the master could hold back no longer. He reared his head against the pillow and grasped John's back.

Electric bolts shot through him as he released his load between their bodies. John held him as he spasmed and shook, kissing his neck and pushing his hips to milk out every drop. Trenton gasped and panted, trying to regain his breath and composure.

John's cock throbbed as he held Trenton. He pushed himself onto his hands and looked down as Trenton gazed into the sea of green. Without a word, John collected the sticky fluid covering their torsos into his hand and rubbed it against his straining cock. He then placed the gooey remnants against Trenton's hole, pushing a finger in to stretch him. "May I, Trent? I want to be inside you."

Trenton lay there, still panting, but his dick stiffened at the proposal before him. With effort, he hooked his arms under his legs and pulled them up to give John access. "Take me."

John smiled and gave him a quick kiss. "I'll be gentle."

"Thank you." Fear raced across his consciousness. Only his former friend, Jonesy, had penetrated him. They'd made love while they were away at school every chance they got for three years until they graduated. Jonesy married Lord Covington's daughter and he no longer wanted anything to do with Trenton.

John lined up and pushed in. A jolt of pain stabbed deep at the master as John's cock filled his body. John was thicker by far than Jonesy, and Trenton struggled to accommodate his larger size. John held still as Trenton grew accustomed to the stretching he received.

Once Trenton's pain subsided, pleasure pushed through in slow crashing waves, eventually replacing any discomfort. He pushed himself against John's pelvis to complete his impalement. John grinned and began a gyrating pumping motion.

Soon, John pounded furiously as Trenton stroked his hardness and moaned, squeezing the thick pole inside him with each thrust. John's pace became frantic, and he stiffened as he released his pent-up desire inside Trenton with an animalistic howl.

John collapsed onto Trenton's body, kissing his neck between pants and gasps. He softened and slipped out of Trenton's hole and rolled to the side.

Trenton gasped at the sudden emptiness. "We aren't finished, are we?"

"No, Trent. I would enjoy being inside you again."

Trenton rolled on top of him, pushing his legs apart with his knees and grinding against John. "How about I get inside of you?"

John's brow furrowed, but his arms wrapped around Trenton's back, pulling him closer to him. "I've not had anyone do that to me before."

Trenton's cock stiffened at the thought of fucking a virgin. "I would be honored to be your first."

John paused. Fear flashed in his eyes. "Please be gentle, Trent."

Trenton smiled. "I promise." He leaned down and brushed his lips against John's in a gentle kiss. "I want to give you as much pleasure as you gave me." Trenton moved forward over John's torso and pressed his hardness against John's mouth. "Prepare me."

John's tongue swirled around the hood on Trenton's cock, then pushed inside and probed against his head. His lips closed around the shaft and began sucking. Pleasure exploded across

Trenton's body. John's hands were everywhere at once, stroking and caressing his frame. He'd never experienced such intense pleasure and intimacy with anyone else as he felt with John. Jonesy had enjoyed the sex, but wasn't interested in emotional attachment. How he wished that John's social class were the same as his, though in many ways this made things easier. As his footman, John would be expected to spend time with Trenton. No one needed to know exactly what they did during that time.

He thrust his erection into John's mouth, reveling in the sensations and shuddering as pleasure rippled through him. John gagged, and Trenton pulled back. "I'm sorry."

John grabbed on to his ass. "No, I want to take you completely. I need a few tries though." He pulled Trenton forward and made several more attempts before he was able to nuzzle his nose into the hair at the root of Trenton's cock.

Trenton pulled off, panting and trying to keep from exploding. John was bringing him to the edge of orgasm, and he wanted to save that. He leaned forward and kissed John again, and then kissed his way down his abdomen. He pushed John's legs up again and darted his tongue into John's hairy entrance.

John's body stiffened and he let out a loud moan. "Oh, sir, no one's done that to me before."

Trenton wasn't sure what possessed him to do it either. If he'd thought about it, he'd have been repulsed and wouldn't have done it. He was grateful for clean flesh and enjoyed the slightly musky scent emanating from between John's legs. He probed farther, leaving as much saliva as possible to ease his entrance. John's body went into spasms as he pulled his legs against his chest, giving Trenton easier access. Trenton would be sure not to do this when they were in the main house, as John's moans would be heard throughout the manor.

His erection pulsing, Trenton pushed himself up and peeled

back the skin to reveal his glistening head, still wet from John's attentions and his own fluid leaking out. He pressed the tip against John's waiting hole and pushed in.

John gasped and put one hand against Trenton's chest. "Hold it there."

Trenton didn't move, though the exquisite tightness surrounding his cock made waiting excruciating. "Set the pace, darling boy. I want this to be pleasurable for both of us."

John's face scrunched up, his eyes shut tight. He took in deep breaths and then pushed against Trenton's hardness. Trenton put his hand on John's chest and pinched his nipple. John's eyes flew open and his hole relaxed, allowing more of Trenton to enter him. "My God, Trent, that is amazing."

"This is just the beginning." Trenton pushed forward and slowly impaled John the rest of the way. He paused when he bottomed out, reveling in the warmth and pressure around his shaft. When John moved, Trenton needed all of his willpower not to erupt.

He set a rhythmic motion, sliding in and out in slow pumps. John wrapped his legs around Trenton's torso and clutched the sheets with his hands. His eyes were closed again and his mouth hung open, an occasional moan escaping from between his lips.

The constant tightness brought Trenton to the brink of orgasm. He had to stop to hold off his imminent explosion. "Roll onto your stomach." John's eyes flew open as Trenton pulled out of him.

Once on his stomach, John spread his legs. Trenton took a moment to admire the smooth pale skin, perfect and unblemished, spread before him. He ran his hands along the bottom's legs and up to massage his back.

John groaned. "That is remarkable. Please, I want you inside me again."

Trenton smiled as he moved his body along John. "Your wish is my command." His prick slid along the crevasse and found the waiting entrance. He thrust deep and entered him in one fluid motion. John clutched the pillow and bit into it as Trenton fucked him hard.

Trenton again neared the point of release and backed out. John whimpered at the sudden exit. "Turn back over, beautiful man; I want to see the pleasure on your face as I fill you."

John flipped back over and again pulled his legs to his chest. Trent entered him and thrust hard, his desire burning at the cries and moans of his lover. The pleasure built up quickly. When he could no longer hold back, he increased his speed, his mind registering only lust and pleasure. He leaned forward and clamped his hands onto John's shoulders. Gazing into this man's beautiful eyes, he rammed deep one last time and roared his release. John's back arched and his shaft exploded, covering his chest and stomach with his load.

Trenton collapsed on top of him, and John wrapped his arms around Trenton's waist. Between heaving breaths and shuddering aftershocks, he planted small kisses on John's neck. John's head nestled against his shoulder. After a few moments, he rolled off John and onto his side.

John put one arm under his head and stretched out the other onto the pillow next to Trenton. "I'm a bit of a mess."

Exhaustion and contentment settled over Trenton as he scooted closer to John. He was finding it difficult to keep his eyes open. "It doesn't matter right now."

Side by side on the bed, Trenton draped his arm over John's chest, kissing the pale skin of his torso. He put his head against the outstretched arm below him.

John turned his head and kissed Trenton's forehead. "Was I to your liking, sir?"

Trenton pushed himself up and leaned on his elbow to look down into John's eyes with a smile. "Trent."

John grinned as he reached up and caressed Trenton's cheek. "Sorry. Trent."

Trenton stood before Lord Pennington's formidable frame in his drawing room. "I'm sorry, Father, but I cannot marry Miss Meikle. I have no interest in her, and, though I understand your business with her father, I have no intention of being a pawn pushed across a chessboard of your design."

His father's disdainful eyes looked him up and down. "You're brother is already married."

Trenton stiffened. "And he's miserable. If he's not careful, one of the maids will be with child."

His father sighed. "Then what is it you want, boy?"

"I'm ready to travel. I want to see the world and then come back and run the estate."

Lord Pennington crossed his arms. "Is that so?"

"Yes, Father."

The two men held each other's gaze until Lord Pennington smiled and put a fatherly hand on Trenton's shoulder. "At last you've become a man. Where will you travel to?"

"Amsterdam and then on to Russia."

"Interesting. Take your footman with you. He'll make a good traveling companion. I'm aware that young John wishes to broaden his own horizons. You'll both make many discoveries along the way."

Trenton smiled. They already had.

"Like father like son, eh?" Gavin Brownlie, footman to Lord Pennington, said as he sipped his afternoon tea.

John chuckled, stirring sugar into his own cup. "You'd know."

"Indeed. His Lordship was a tiger in the sack. Definitely worth the month it took to get him there." He put his cup down on the small table in their shared room. "Did he like you?"

"I think so. I played the 'never been taken' bit on him. Turned his crank, sure enough. He doesn't need to know that you and I sleep in the same bed."

"Or *don't* sleep, eh?" Gavin smirked. "So what now?"

"He wants me to meet him at the Lodge again tomorrow."

"Well done. I knew he'd be like his old man. They's like two peas in a pod."

John sat back, his mind wandering to his afternoon with Trenton. His cock grew in his trousers as a pleasant warmth settled into his body. "Mind you, I did quite enjoy it. He's a fine man." He winked at Gavin. "And he'll inherit this manor house some day."

Gavin checked his pocket watch. "We don't have to be back on duty for another two hours. Fancy a bit of fun?"

"Of course. I have to keep your ass stretched open to take his Lordship's thick cock, don't I?" He set his cup onto the table and stood. Their clothes quickly fell away and John sank to his knees. He sucked on Gavin's stiffening erection.

"Oh, mate, no one sucks like you. What am I going to do when you go away to Amsterdam?"

John stood and pushed them both onto the bed. He spat onto his dick and lined up to enter his friend. "Don't worry. I learned my techniques from Trenton's brother, William. Maybe he can keep you busy while I'm away."

# FOLLY'S DITCH

Felice Picano

My Lord,

From just outside of Croydon-town north to London is not far, and while fatigue soon approached my walking thither, so did an elderly farmer—nearly asleep, driving a dray that was laden high with split-ricks of horse feed—who offered me a ride. I could not help but note that all the while he looked carefully at my face and my theatrical costume. The former was still not free of the greasepaint of the night's performance, and the latter rather more elegantly turned out than is common, or so I'd wager, among those he might be expected to regularly encounter at so small an hour upon the road.

I explained my predicament as well as I might, which gained his laughter and eventual help.

He left me near the King's Yard in Deptford, where his business of the morn lay, and there he was good enough to arrange for me to travel onward farther than I might have dared hope, through Upper Kent, upon an acquaintance's dogcart, and up to Halfway House. Once arrived, I was dropped off, tipped the fellow a penny, and was left to my own devices.

Although I'd often asked, as we encountered others coming against us on the roads or whenever we made a stop, no one had seen the one I sought. So it was, with a growing sad belief that I had lost forever those so ambivalent charms, that at sunrise I took to my tuppence bed at Halfway House, that noted inn.

I awakened late at noon and was immediately assailed by two strong odors: one, quite unpleasant and due to the retraction of the Thames River tide, only several streets distant; the other an equally strong and thus countervailingly delicious aroma of Arabian coffee being brewed. From the little height of the inn's placement, I might look across the flats of East Rotherhite to the Thames's largest bend south, and across it to the India Docks and Isle of Dogs. So I found myself quite near to London itself, the place of my birth and of my earliest years, as I made my way downstairs to the public room below.

Even so, it was very different a scene from the one that I'd appreciated only a day earlier—I mean the deep green lawns and flowered country lanes about the town of Croydon—and I must have sighed rather more theatrically than my new companions were accustomed to hearing. Indeed, our view now was of a gray and rainy day. Sleet in slow gales crossed the face of the mullioned windows. The vista they gave upon, even on the best of days, was, however, oppressive: miles of double-story dock-side warehouses. The river presented its least prepossessing prospect here, and upon its other bank lay only more of the same dreary warehousing, interspersed with thrown-together hovels and other constructions of iron used I supposed for lading.

"Cheer up, lad," the slavey in her food-stained apron said. "Since you had coin, you'll break fast well here at Halfway

House. Fresh-baked bread, Irish pertaters baked and topped in a buttered slab, three fat toasted rashers, and a half slice of tomater; what do you say also to a egg?"

I said that it sounded to be a Lupercalian feast, and soon sat down to it all.

Imagine my astonishment, if you will, when several minutes later I had only just wiped the egg off my chin, and who should saunter down the stairs and into the public room but a lanky fellow with hair as orange as one of those Spanish mandarins that I know your Lordship to be so partial to.

Though youthful, he had the casual yet elegant air that declared that he was living off five hundred a year in Railroad Shares. He also possessed a voice, that once heard, I could never forget.

"'Ere now, me blandished female of pulchritude," says the newcomer in greeting to the semi-stupefied lass pouring him coffee. "I'll need as large a repast as possible this day."

In vain did she offer him her bill of fare: kippers, herring, potatoes and tomatoes. He waved them off with a "Fer mere riffraff." Eggs, bread, bacon and ham also were dismissed out of hand. He had had "a regular laborious night of it," averred he, and what he wished—his gray-blue eyes all aglitter—was nothing less than a "beefsteak with all the trimmins. And don't yer skimp on the gravy none."

After she had left for the larder, he smelt his coffee and sipped it as though he were the grandest Turk among the Ottomans. He had made short work of it when he deigned to notice myself quite openly staring at him. He then cocked one flame-colored eyebrow over a suddenly inquisitive eye.

"Do I *know* you, sir?" he asked, loudly, and in the most provocative tone of voice possible to the otherwise empty taproom.

"I believe you *do* know me, sir!" I responded, equally aggrieved.

Now his two burning bright eyebrows fought for which one might reach his hairline first, so irate and perplexed was he.

"Have we had...*words*, sir?" he asked, fuming.

"Upon a time, we did indeed have words...and slept together, too. Arm in arm, legs pressed against each other," I added, saucily.

He retained his surprisingly cool demeanor, especially after having been given such extreme provocation.

"Indeed, sir, you are extremely young to afford the services that are provided by Mr. Alistair MacIlhenny, the Third."

Here he peered at me closely.

It was all I could do not to burst into laughter.

"Perhaps so, sir." I replied. "But at the time, your sleeping services went for less than nothing, as you were yourself so young." As he blinked at me, I added, "And, sir, you were at that time hailed by the name of Lobster Tail."

He all but knocked over his coffee cup. "Yer don't say so! Then art yer one of the Grimmins Lads? I thought yer face familiar, albeit too clean for any certain identification."

He stood up and approached my table. "Let me guess, Little Tomallalley, is it? Or rather Lil' Tarpon? Wait! I know who? That voice!" He pretended to ponder, listening to some invisible interlocutor. "Ne'er Cockney; always a bit larned." He turned to me in triumph. "Tis Scallop. Why, Scallop, it is, t'isn't it?"

Here we both rose and clasped hands and shoulders, and he joined me at my deal table where he explained neither his alias nor a great deal else, at least not immediately.

I drank more coffee while his meal (more apt for evening than morning) arrived, and as he tucked into it, I was once more taken by how such a slender lad could put away such large quantities of food. He had done so as a boy, taking four meat pies, not two like the rest of us Grimmins lads, and two fat brown loaves, not one, and always making fast work of them.

We exchanged our histories—or at least in my case a somewhat expurgated version of the same. Here, across the river from London-town, it had already become evident to me that should I ever perchance come across The Person whom I'd lost it would be completely circumstantial. In a city of a half-million souls, that someone was as lost to me as a ha'penny at the Seven Dials crossroads.

"Then yer cannot return to the te-atter?" MacIlhenny said more than asked, after I had explained my predicament.

"Not that theatre, at least. Certainly not. And who knows but in a few weeks time the word will have gotten about of my...*misadventure*, and I shall be barred from all such establishments."

"'Tis a shame," Lobster Tail declared with a frown. "I do like a good play, mesself, and I would've so enjoyed seeing yer tread the boards all costumed up as a Pirate or Maid. But as yer now unemployed and I suppose seeking some of the same, p'raps I may have a proposition to dangle afore yer?" said he.

"I am eager to hear," said I. "Are you self employed?"

"Nay, but that I am *well employed*." He looked about to see that no one was listening, then added conspiratorially, "by none other than Tiger Jukes!"

"Tiger Jukes?"

"Not so loud. Not so loud. The Tige prefers to be known but not well known, if you see what I mean."

I didn't but shook my head just the same. "In what capacity?"

"Rum."

"Rum to drink?"

"Aye, some of that, but all of what Tiger Jukes operates and manages is damnably rum!"

By which I gathered that Tiger Jukes was a master criminal of sorts, and Lobster Tail now one of his gang of crime-fellows.

"In what capacity?" I repeated with real interest.

"Why, Tige's got the 'extras' of the docks sewed up tight, does Tige. From China Hall to Jamaica Row and all of the docks of The Driff in betwixt, not one single spot of cargo is pilfered but Tiger Jukes isn't behind it or doesn't receive a percentage of it."

"And this is how you eat beefsteaks for breakfast?" asked I.

"Well, never mind I, Scallop me lad. Yer shall be eatin' them soon enough. I shall take yer to Tiger Jukes mesself."

There was the little matter of him paying his tariff, which Lobs settled by grandly saying, "The genl'mun upstairs shall pay it all. As usual."

Laughing at my befuddlement at this mystery, he grasped my arm and led me forth.

We strode on in the decreased drizzle, two great lads, well fed, and with pence in our pocket—pounds carried I, wrapped tightly beneath my more naturally acquired prized possessions—toward where could be made out Wapping, across the turbid waters. The rain had abated only a little by then.

There, in a neighborhood not extremely different from that we had just left, if more ancient, seemingly erected during the time of Charles the Murdered King, we came upon those mansions, somewhat the worse for wear from the eternal southerly winds that blew off Jacob's Island, and known as Folly's Ditch.

Amid the twists and turns of the various lanes, one larger and somewhat more restored edifice rose upon Rope Lane and Rotherhite Road. Before this better-looking establishment three Bravos idled, coming to stand tall once we had approached across the lane. Recognizing my companion, they sat themselves down again and proceeded to idle once more, playing mumble-the-peg and swearing at the results.

"'El-lo, Mac," said the tallest, roughest and most scarred of the three, an Irishman of so snub a nose that one might roll coins upon it and they would gather but not fall. He was of hair so strong and straight and black that were it not for his high complexion and green eyes one might take him for a Portaguee.

"'El-lo, Dunphy. Is the Tige up and about?" Lobs asked.

"Holding a usual levee, Mac." Then looking me over, "Who's this then?"

"A friend."

"A doss lad, you mean to say."

"I said a friend," MacIlhenny insisted.

Dunphy moved back, but as I passed in through the foyer, said, "Ye'll be dining on Irish sausage yet." Which I thought an excellent prophecy, as I was partial to sausages.

In any case, the restored grandeur of the exterior of this manse was duplicated within, and soon we had arrived at a curved stairway dropping down into a fleur-de-lis-papered hall. There sat a heavily painted and cheerful woman, her figure all but hidden in a gigantic flowery chintz pelisse, her high hair all but secreted within dozens of paper curlers. She sat at a fine, almost spindly, French-looking table upon which tea in bone china and half-eaten pasties were placed.

Several men were seated in chairs before her or standing and listening to her, carefully, as her voice was low and rather sweet. My companion held me in the rear of the crowded room, only crooking a finger when she happened to look in our direction. At which time I noticed a lovely pair of large, almost saucy, black eyes, and the once pert features of a soubrette as she looked my self over.

As they all spoke in a low tone of voice, all I might make out were various expressions of astonishment and dismay from the men, while she remained ever level and even toned. At last their business was concluded and the fellows all made for the exit.

She now crooked a finger at us, and Mac pushed me forward.

"Mrs. Athaliah Jukes," said she, swanning toward me a not unattractive hand. She made a moue, and I knelt to buss her chubby pink hand.

"Mr. Addison Grimmins," I introduced myself, causing Mac to let out and then suppress a laugh.

"Please sit, Mister Grimmins," she said, offering me, but not Lobster Tail, a seat. It was he whom she addressed, however. "Dear young Mister MacIlhenny, it does my heart much good to see that you have taken my advice into your ordinarily heedless head and have at long last brought to me someone who may do great good for us all, and who may make both my and his own fortune."

I thought this a good opening and was about to speak when she placed a perfumed finger across my lips and continued on to him.

"We know that your own attributes, Mister MacIlhenny, are, while few in number, centered upon...a prodigality of nature!"

She giggled while my friend colored.

"But whatever young Mister Grimmins's own male attributes may be is of far less moment to us, whatsoever, since he is of a personal beauty, of a—may I put it?— *classical* beauty that I have not seen in this house since that moment when I myself was fortunate enough to be carried across that threshold. Upon my wedding day, young sirs. By the late Mister Jukes. And shortly thereafter had that portrait taken."

Her hand pointed to an upper wall of the hall. There I made out a portrait which might be construed as herself, quite young, half settled upon a settee of pink satin, while at her feet several black pugs in beige paw-shoes sat.

"He has come to join us in our quieter dock-work," MacIlhenny now said, in a tight voice.

She flounced up to her feet and once risen she proved to be unexpectedly large and most rotund.

"No. No. *NO. NO!* You're *quite* mistaken, Mister MacIlhenny. Quite! Does one *toss* a rare Brazilian orchid into the *gutters* of Rope *Lane*? Of course not, Mister Grimmins—may I call you Addison?" she simpered into my face. "Whatever Mister MacIlhenny so monstrously *intended* by introducing us, I am able to assure you that I have in mind a far greater destiny for you."

"Not...a doss lad?" he all but strangled out the words.

"May I remind you," she said grandly, yet firmly, "that *you* have been and still are a doss lad, and if I must say so, one of the most *popular* in the history of this house. Perhaps," she added darkly, "it is time that you should quit that occupation yourself—to your *youngers* and betters—and move on to other labors more like quiet dock-work."

"I meant..." Mac had paled somewhat. "I'd prefer not."

"Naturally, you would prefer not," she said. "And so I supposed. Yet, tell me, Mister MacIlhenny, how much were your earnings yester day and night?"

"Three shillings, four pence."

He held it out, and she promptly took the coins and dropped them down into her décolletage.

"And yet, Mister MacIlhenny, I recall a date in the not so recent past when your prodigal gifts were wont to bring in six shillings per day—regularly."

"I also had a large meal," he added, somewhat shamefacedly.

"However, neither *I* nor this house did share in that meal," she said, "and so it is immaterial."

She waved him off, and he retired to a corner of the large chamber, where I heard him throwing a knife into an old chest.

She, meanwhile, spent the next ten minutes doing her best to charm me.

I would remain in the house, she told me, and never—like my friend—need go out of doors upon "calls," she added. Naturally enough I would have all the time in the world to myself when not at the house and much freedom, and two, no, *three* full suits of brand new clothing, all bespoke down to my undergarments. I would dine like the Duke of Bedford and...

"Doing what?" I thought to ask. "That is, for what would I be paid, ma'am?"

"Not very much work at all as far as the actual labor goes," she replied, glibly enough. "And certainly not as much as if you were a quiet dock worker, which can, at times, after all, be extremely hard work, and at other times even perilous work as it is, you understand, a species of pilferage." She giggled and then darted another question at me. "You possess how many years, young Addison?"

"More than enough," said I.

She merely smiled, rather coyly I might add. "Then you shall have seven, perhaps eight excellent earning years. And because of your *gift*, we shall split your take down the middle."

I heard Lobster Tail snort something from within his niche.

"*Down the middle.* Since," she now said, loudly, "I shall easily be able to charge *double* the ordinary fee, given your... *visage*, Addison. It's evident that only the highest born and most well off shall ever *see* your face, my boy, or indeed *know* of your existence in this house. Why, by the termination of seven years, you may have earned hundreds, indeed probably thousands of pounds."

It all sounded most promising, but I still didn't know what I would be doing, and asked her once more.

"Well, it's rather an indelicate subject for a lady to expatiate upon. But your friend shall do so..." She then turned to Lobs. "You do know, Mister MacIlhenny, don't you, that Bishop Huddlestone is scheduled to be here in a few minutes. Go to your regular chamber and prepare for him as usual. And while doing so, why not place our young friend in that side closet, the one with the grilled doorway, so he may see exactly how you have yourself fared so very well to date in my employ, and thus how it will be that his own fortune may soon be obtained."

"Come closer one brief moment, Addison," said she, and when I did she took my hands, commenting, "Like a gentleman's." And then she touched my cheeks, adding, "Like those of a babe in arms."

Lobster Tail took his leave of her, sulky, with a poor grace, shuffling his lank body upstairs, and looking back to see if I was following.

"Catch him up, Addison!" Athaliah Jukes advised. I could now hear her counting coin upon the table below us.

We ascended to street level and then up one more, and only then did I make out how large the house was, especially its many doors to varied chambers on the top two landings. On each some fellow lurked, and, even by daylight, burning spermaceti oil might be sweetly smelt from within the various lanterns ensconced upon the hallway walls.

From my view of the stairways and corridors, the house appeared furnished very handsomely with a surfeit of furniture and furnishings both, with pictures and marble busts upon plinths, and handsomely patterned papered walls. To tell the truth, I already liked this better than being about the docks in all weather.

More puzzling, however, than the many and various chambers, was that each such door held at eye level a brass plaque about the width of a man's hand, and within it, in some fanciful design, the cursively detailed name of a single month of the year.

Lobster Tail entered into the second such, April, while I followed.

Like the hallways, the chamber was well furnished and well warmed by a small fireplace. It contained a quite large bed, canopied over in olden style, with a commode at one end and a backless chair that stood nearby. A window, small and high, provided a glimpse of the still inclement daylight out of doors.

"What shall you do here?" I asked.

"Receive a visitor," he replied, surly. He then pointed to what appeared to be an adjoining closet, closed off by a wooden work grill. "In there goes yer fer the duration of my visit. Watch carefully and so yer copies whatever yer sees fer yer own edication," he added, pointing at my chest.

I entered the adjoining cabinet and found a small wooden stool where I myself would sit to witness what I guessed would be some kind of criminal activity: picking pockets, or lambasting, or...who knows what? My mind was aflutter with so many exciting possibilities.

Before closing the fretted gate, I asked, "Still, Lobs, you never said. Where is Tiger Jukes?"

"*She* is Tiger Jukes," he replied, looking downward from where we had just come. "The greedy bitch! Or hadn't yer figured it yet?"

Imagine then my surprise when Lobs removed most of his clothing and lay himself upon his back upon the bedsheets.

Quickly enough, a timid knock on the door revealed his

visitor, who stepped in, looking flushed and yet excited: a man of near sixty years of age, distinguished and even holy in both his mien and in his garb.

By this time, Lobster had taken up a small piece of reading matter, a blue-paper-covered book no bigger than his hand, and he was perusing its pages, as though utterly unaware of anything as common as a visitor.

And while he may have been unaware, one could not say the same for his male member—so exposed within that expanse of reddish-brown lawn—which immediately stood itself up taller. I imagined this visitor must be Bishop Huddlestone. He quietly as a mouse removed his coat—a large pale Ulster, against the wet—and he bent down at one end of the bed as though in prayer. Covering his mouth, he tittered once, and then began to utter words difficult for me to ascertain, but which evidently Lobster Tail's member was familiar with, as it now erected itself to a great height as though some living object, and at the same time filled itself out sideways as well, flushing red. And all the while Lobster read on, making much of turning a page, and seemed unconscious of it or of his visitor.

Even from my impaired station, I could make out the Bishop's fingers reaching forward toward that large, increasingly ruddy object. But instead he satisfied himself with patting the surrounding hair and drawing the lightest of invisible lines upon the adjoining muscles and quite visible blue veins as though mapping out the territory. Quickly enough, one hand had gone round the Bishop's neck and removed a silken scarf of the most blazing carmine dye, and this he carefully arranged around Lobster's manhood, careful to enclose the paler orange accompanying sack. Was that Latin I heard Huddlestone uttering as he crept closer by inches to the desired object, gingerly, as though expecting at any moment to be pushed away?

No sooner was the adored thing wrapped about and singled out than it was oh so lightly stroked by quivering Bishopric fingertips until it grew quite red, upon which the still chanting Episcopal bent over and adjoined to those tips the pointed tip of his tongue. There it dandled and darted and made tiny little forays all over the now glistening object, which quite resembled a warrior's helmet, until it was I supposed fully widened and filled out.

Several minutes more of this finger and tongue play continued—and Lobster all the while seemingly unaware and enthralled by his true-murder-mystery story—until the Bishop could no longer resist and fell upon it all the way until a portion of it had quite disappeared into the maw of his priestly mouth. There the Bishop worked upon it using hands, tongue and mouth, all the while I swear muttering Latin homilies.

This went on for some time, until, suddenly, Lobster dropped his little booklet to one side and, using both largish hands, he held that sacred white-haired head until it was utterly still. As I looked on, I noticed my friend's head suddenly fall backward, eyes up to the ceiling, and at the same time I saw his entire midsection, flat rear end and all, arise, I attest, at least two inches off the bedsheets.

When he subsided back to them again a few minutes later, it was with the heaviest exhalation, one from the very deepest part of him.

At this turn of events, the Bishop forbore from his ministrations, backed away slowly, unwrapped the scarf, sniffed it quickly, stuffed it into his waistcoat, then arose to stand, muttering more garbled Latin all the while. Once he'd buttoned his trousers and his waistcoat, he made some kind of hand-figured blessing over Lobster's supine body. Grasping his Ulster, he then turned and rushed out.

Silence reigned in that chamber for the longest time.

Suddenly, MacIlhenny rose up in bed and looked quickly at his member, which he dabbled at lightly with one finger.

"And so now, me Scallop-lad, yer have witnessed what 'tis that a doss lad does to earn his living."

I slipped out of hiding. "How many times per diem?" I asked.

"How many times per...whut?"

"Each day?" I asked.

"How many times could yer?" he asked, somewhat perplexed at my question.

"Three. Four. More," I assured him.

He looked at me more closely. "I took thee for a country lad in manners."

"Hardly so, old Lobs. I've been with a traveling theatre troupe. The Invincibles, man and maid, taught me quickly enough and fully enough, too, how to pleasure a fellow within their caravans at nightfall."

"To have it done to yer?" he asked.

"Naturally. By maid *and* man. And also..." I teased.

"And also to do it yerself?" he then asked in some surprise. "For there, me Scallop Lad, lies the true earnings of this doss lad trade, though yer must never say so to the fat one down the stairs."

"Naturally, enough, Lobs, old fellow. To do so oneself is *all* the art. And in the theatre, one learns to *always* aim to please through art."

He took a while to absorb that information while he got dressed and tied on his shoes.

"Well, then, Scallop Lad," he said, arising now and beginning to put on his waistcoat, "I recognize that 'tis time fer me to seek another place. Or p'raps to retire from the field altogether."

"But why? Cannot we operate in tandem, or as a team?"

"Nay, Scallop. With yer looks and yer experience, yer fortune is indeed here, as Tige fore-omened, inside this house. And upon fine, fat sausages and beefsteaks both shall yer dine!" he added. "Whilst I am, as yer've seen yerself, naught but a one-trick pony."

And though I tried to dissuade him, he would not listen, and in a few days, as I settled in, he left our criminal mistress's employ.

I asked Dunphy and the other house guards if they ever saw him about the docks, doing light-fingered work there, but they said no.

Yet another smooth-faced scholar who paid well to merely kiss my pink and white bottom while he flogged his member, told me once that he believed my old compatriot had "gone the reformed whore's way." He swore that during the baptism of a well-off family, where he'd accompanied his aged mother, he'd come upon MacIlhenny's inimitably lanky form clad in the ebony garb of a church deacon. He was silently presiding along-side higher Episcopals at one of our larger cathedrals. And so, I supposed, my friend had found a way in which to satisfy his *and* his client-Lord's inclinations.

Upon his leaving Folly's Ditch, I became, albeit briefly, the highest-paid doss lad ever for Tiger Jukes, and as word of my charms spread, eventually the highest paid and most sought after in all of London-town.

But the remainder of my history, my Lord, I believe you already know. As you were my client in that house, my most generous and my most particular one—and my eventual savior. And for that, I thank ye.

Your servant, Addison Grimmins

# MANOR GAMES

## Michael Roberts

I say," he said.

"Sir?" I inquired.

"Dash it all," he elaborated, "I've...and he's...and so...well, *you know*."

"I'm afraid I don't," I said.

"Kensington-Ffoulke," he blurted.

"Ah," said I. Actually, I wouldn't have known he said "Kensington-Ffoulke" if I hadn't known he said "Kensington-Ffoulke." Kensington-Ffoulke's name, after all, does not come trippingly off the tongue or into the ear.

But I knew Kensington-Ffoulke; he was one of three men with whom my master, Jeremy, played cards every week. Like Jeremy, the three owned substantial acreages of land on the English countryside, with opulent mansions that, I thought, were designed to ostentatiously mirror the owners' fortunes. Kensington-Ffoulke's residence, for example, looked as if he thought he were Henry VIII rather than an admittedly powerful

English aristocrat at the turn of the twentieth century. I could never understand why he chose to become one of Jeremy's associates unless it was because Kensington-Ffoulke, who was constructed something like a bull elephant (although perhaps more alluring), was drawn to someone he could bully and bluster into acquiescence.

In any case, given my master's lack of skill at playing cards, he was usually in debt to Kensington-Ffoulke, and usually substantially in debt. And whereas some men would have forgiven the debt, or have let my master play indefinitely on credit (and thereby probably increased the debt tenfold), that was not in Kensington-Ffoulke's nature. No, as my master's obligations mounted, so did Kensington-Ffoulke's insistence that he be paid. And any chance that Jeremy might simply stop playing with the three men was not feasible, as Kensington-Foulke would not have allowed such an escape.

The other two men fared better because they were, to be quite honest, better card players than my master (which, to be quite honest, wasn't really saying all that much). They were, incidentally, appealing young men somewhere between my master and Kensington-Ffoulke in construction.

(It is very tiresome to repeat Kensington-Ffoulke's name—although he was adamant that he be called his name fully, being proud of the heritage that culminated in that name—so I will refer to him simply as K.)

Of late, K had been progressively more vocal in his pursuit of payment, often and loudly. And considering his size, his obvious strength and his reputation, it was probably prudent not to ignore his demands.

But my master was not, shall we say, financially grounded, and he couldn't accumulate enough funds to satisfy K, so it became increasingly likely that K was going to at last explode and wreak some havoc upon my master, and probably some substantial havoc.

My master was, of course, reluctant to have that happen. As was I, to be sure.

"But I don't know how—" he said. "And so of course—" Then he paused and stared at me most piteously—a look to which I was not unaccustomed, to be candid. Although I was barely two years older than his twenty-three, he regarded me, as he regards me still, as a wiser guide through the difficulties of life—which for him seem many and varied. I am his man-of-all-trades, and he depends upon me as if I were simultaneously an equal and a part, an essential part, of his staff. And now once more we were at an occasion that required my skills.

So, I thought.

I certainly couldn't defend my master physically. I am a slight man, even more slight than he. It seems quite possible that a heavy wind could lift him up and transport him to another continent. He is a very attractive man, but he looks rather as if he should be a schoolmaster instead of one of the landed gentry. And so I knew that I had to rely upon something other than brute force. But what was the solution to this problem?

I could furnish my master with no financial assistance, since, after all, my existence was dependent upon him. And even though there were times when he could pay me no salary, at least I was domiciled and fed (and well-domiciled, to be sure). And I did like Jeremy, though perhaps (I wasn't sure) not quite just in a master-servant fashion.

After I had thought some more, the answer flashed in my mind in one of those sudden bursts of inspiration to which I have become accustomed.

"Sir," I said, "at your game tonight, before your guests arrive, I shall secret myself beneath the table."

"Which table?" he asked.

"The one on which you play cards, sir." It is sometimes (often) necessary to be as specific as possible in discussing things with my master. "As I said, I shall secret myself beneath the table, on which you must put some sort of large cloth that will conceal my presence. Then at the appropriate moment—"

"At the appropriate moment, what?" he asked breathlessly.

"I shall *distract* him, sir."

"How will you do that?"

"Well, let us say that my tongue is agile."

"What?"

"My lips are supple."

"What?"

"My mouth can draw men to the pinnacle of gratification."

"I say, what?"

"I give good head, sir."

"Oh. Oh! *Oh?*"

"Yes. I don't mean to boast, but let us say that after I administer my talents to Kensington-Ffoulke, he will not be in a position to efficiently play the game, let alone win, and I daresay that with luck—with luck *and* my abilities—you can win back what you owe him and perhaps actually exceed that amount and have him owing you."

"Hmm. You'd be willing to do that for me?"

"Yes, sir."

"You're a very generous man."

"I know, sir."

He considered my offer.

"Well," he said, "I don't suppose that the situation can get any worse."

"No, sir."

"And it might indeed get better."

"It will, sir. Have I ever steered you wrong?"

"No. All right, Tompkins"—for that is my name—"you may carry out your scheme. And good luck to us both."

On the evening of the card game, the master and the cook and I prepared the hors d'oeuvres earlier than usual. We set up the food and the cards and the other accoutrements for the games. I squatted down and crawled beneath the table and sat in a cross-legged manner I had learned from an ashram in Tunisia, and Jeremy covered the table and me with a cloth that touched the floor.

Then I waited.

I didn't know what the master was doing, though I heard indefinite movements around me. Perhaps it was simply nervous puttering.

The card players arrived: Smythe-Smith, then the Duke of Earle, and lastly, I could tell by his blustery entrance, Kensington-Ffoulke.

"Well, tonight I'm going to win even more from you than I have before," trumpeted K, "and tonight you are going to pay me all of the money—all of the large sum of money—you owe me. Have I made myself clear?"

I heard my master answer, but I couldn't tell what he was saying, the volume of his response was so low, and I understood that it was impossible for him to match K's overbearing, intimidating comportment.

The four men sat down.

I gave them several minutes to get involved in the game. K was smoking one of his noxious cigars, and as the smoke drifted down, I hoped that I wouldn't be attacked by a fit of coughing and give away our strategy.

Finally, I looked around at the four sets of legs spread before me. Yes, there was my target.

With all of the skill I had acquired during my safecracking days, I gently undid the trousers that were now directly before me, and then lightly reached with two fingers to undo the button in the underwear fly. A cock plopped out as if it had been waiting for me to set it free.

It was a long and lean cock, and I took a moment to appreciate its dimensions before I lifted it and slid it into my waiting mouth.

"Nnnnhhhh?" I heard above me.

"Is something wrong?" one of the men asked.

"No. I don't think so."

I began to track the tender flesh with my tongue.

"Nnnnnhhhh!"

"Are you sure nothing's wrong?"

"No, I...I think I must have been out too long in the cold air, and...and...my throat is...it hurts."

I licked the head of the cock, which was stretching and becoming quite firm.

"Nnhh! Nhhhh! Nnnnnn! Oh, oh, I hope that whatever ailment is...ailing me, I don't transmit it to anyone."

I let the cock out of my mouth and ran my tongue first along the top, then along the bottom. I wished that I could taste the testicles, but extracting them from the undergarment would no doubt prove to be impossible without causing more than a little discomfort to their owner and might instigate his inspection under the table to find what in blazes was happening. So I just licked, up and down, up and down.

"Nnnnn! Hhhhhh!"

I lapped at the head of the cock, which released a drop of moisture onto my tongue.

"Nnnnnhhhhh!"

I thought that it was not going to be necessary to maintain my ministrations much longer, and after I'd taken two more voyages up and down the length of his stiff cock, he said, "Nnnhhhohhhhh!" and flowed into my mouth, thickly, tastily.

At that point, my master's voice came through the cloth. I couldn't understand what he was saying, so I leaned over and put my ear where I thought his face was and said, "What?" and he whispered in reply, "Wrong member! Wrong member!" Which certainly seemed true in more ways than one.

Another man said, "Jeremy, what are you doing?" and my master said, "I thought I dropped something. Oh, here it is, one of the chips."

I was rather proud of my master for inventing an excuse to look under the table that made his actions seem quite plausible. After all, his thinking was frequently not so quick.

The games continued—mine and the one above me.

I regarded the three clad crotches and the dangling penis before me.

I lightly loosened a covering. Extricating this cock would be more difficult because it was askew in the undershorts. Fortunately, the slant was upward as well as to the left. Patiently I prodded the prick toward the fly until just a slight bending was required to push it forward and out.

This cock was not as long as the first, but it was wider, and it provided an appetizing mouthful.

When I took it between my lips, there was a sudden slap of a hand on the table above me.

"Now what's wrong with *you*?" asked one of the men.

"It's...it's...it's a new method of concentration," said the man in front of me. "I've learned that it helps me think better and therefore play the game better if I, well, *slap*."

I encircled the head of this cock with my tongue, dipping into the slit.

There was another, louder slap.

"I wish you'd stop that," said one of the other players.

"I can't. I, uh, don't want to."

I released the cock from my mouth and then did a moist inspection of its heft with my tongue.

*Slap!*

I sort of looped around the cock with my tongue, and then I added a spiral, so that I was going up and over and across at the same time I surveyed the length.

*Slap! Slap!*

"I'm finding it very difficult to concentrate with all of your attacks," said another of the men.

"Well, all of the attacks are...giving me...pleasure. I mean, they're giving me help...*help!*"

There was a trio of slaps as I reabsorbed the cock and ascended and descended with increasing speed.

I tasted a couple of delightful drops of essence, and then there was a shudder that rippled and rolled across his legs and into his crotch and into his cock and then into me as the man orgasmed, pounding the table, feeding a substantial supply of dense juices down my throat.

"Are you quite done?" said an exasperated voice above.

I almost answered in the affirmative myself, but fortunately "Yes" replied my bountiful benefactor. "I...I think I'm...quite done."

"Well, thank heavens!"

"Yes," said my master. "It's been WRONG of you to make so much noise, and the cards you have been playing are WRONG, and your concentration seems not to have been helped except in the WRONG direction."

*Hmm.* I apparently had made another mistake.

I looked at the two remaining veiled crotches, set off by the fleshly parentheses of the double dangling dicks. And I certainly could tell which one was K's nether region. His impressive legs seemed like two trees that had grown together into the sturdily packed pod of his pants. And so with that knowledge, I slid over in front of my next object of sensual assault and with delicate deliberation unbuttoned him. Doing just that made it quite evident how substantial was his presence, because there was a sizable curve of fabric, and it was taut over what lurked within.

With the greatest of care (because I did not, after all, want him lurching to his feet and overturning the table and then overturning me and raining down physical punishment soon thereafter), I opened his undershorts. By minute degrees, I reached inside and touched his appendage, and it was so warm—no, beyond warm, hot—that my fingers seemed to be almost blistered.

I started to ascertain the magnitude of his masculinity, and I couldn't find a beginning or an end or anything in between. His cock plunged down into his drawers, and I of course couldn't follow it to that destination. I was unable to discover anything but warm, pulsating flesh—no sides, no tip, nothing but a globe of a cock, like one of those vast expanses of land that seemed to have no boundaries, just acre after acre to be endlessly explored.

This was a challenge.

By instinct, I had to figure out how to move this colossal cock, hoping that my hands would acquire some sort of extra perception so that I could fasten upon this coiled serpent and arouse its passions. And it *was* shifting, but was it, was I, going anywhere? Evidently my fingers were guided by some intuition beyond what I could ascribe to my usual facility in dealing with dick, and they sensed—I did not sense; they did—that there was a change in texture, a barely discernible alteration in the shape of the fleshly coil. And still I kept inching toward the opening of this somnolent beast.

At last, the head of his cock glided into my fingers and into view, and it was hooded, and I almost feared the results of my actions, waking the creature into who knew what sort of response, what kind of consequences. And yet it was not just that I was (I hoped) helping my master, but also that some latent intensity acted like a magnet, and I could not if I wanted to— and I did not want to—resist the power of this prick.

I willed my hands to stop shaking and I slid the sheath away from the face of the cock, and it was such an expanse of flesh to transport, and the summit revealed seemed so tremendous, that I closed my eyes momentarily and sought to restrain the palpitations of my mind. I then opened my eyes and looked directly at the dick and met it with my lips and caressed it, and so far there was no discernible effect, no solidifying, so to speak.

K's cock was an amalgam of the other two dicks I had sucked, both long and wide, and I stretched my mouth open as far as it would go, and I surrounded the cock, and my lips were spread enough (though just barely enough) to ingest the bulk of his extensive extension.

I swore I could hear the creak of my jaw as I glided up and down his meaty monster. It had an exotic taste, not at all like the other two cocks, and not really like any other cock to which I had devoted my attentions in the past.

It was, thank goodness, and after what seemed an inordinate period of time, enlarging and thus becoming more than I could encase. And I had to try to satisfy him and me by stroking him with my tongue—stroke, stroke, stroke—until I was at once exhausted and exhilarated.

I thought that I could hear sighing or moaning above me. Then alternating with what I hoped were exhalations of arousal, I heard curses. And both sounds grew louder and louder and more rapid. "How did I—?" said K. And "Damn it, why didn't—?" And "Jeremy, how did you suddenly become such a good player?" And "How could I have made so many damned mistakes?" And "I've lost again? I've lost again! Damn it!"

And congruent with the volume and rate at which the sighs and the curses increased was an increase in the expansion of his cock. I thought surely his dick could get no bigger, but it did, longer and more fully packed.

Then it rose so precipitously that it smacked me in the nose, and there was a volcanic rumbling in K's lower extremities, working its way into his cock, which buzzed like an agitated bee against my nostrils, and he moaned loudly for what seemed an interminable time, and I barely got the tip of his dick in my mouth before he finally erupted. I use that word advisedly, because a deluge, a veritable cascade, flooded my mouth in an astounding volume. Actually, I had to swallow twice to keep his torrent from spilling onto my face and my clothes and the floor and possibly onto the grounds of the estate.

Unexpectedly, I felt an upsurge in the shaking and the quivering and quaking, and I prepared myself for another incredible onslaught of his climatic fervor, and then I realized that the upheaval was in my chest and my stomach and in my loins and running down my legs, as I was seized by a storm of passion that threatened to capsize me. Had my mouth been available at that moment, I might have exclaimed in delight, but instead I controlled as well as I could my own exploding and imploding and concentrated on K's fullness gushing into my throat.

At last it was containable, and I savored the final jolt, his and mine, tasting the thick, ripe, fruitful abundance of his masculine explosion. I sat sloshing the succor around in my mouth and gazed at K's cock, still uplifted as if it had more to distribute, as if it were not at all willing to forgo the attention that I had paid to it. I then listened to the conversation above me, which, now that the moaning had trailed away, consisted mainly of K's saying, "How the hell could I do that? How could I lose so much after winning so much? How the hell—?" and so forth.

My master, who seemed only a second away from abandoning himself to unrestrained and possibly frenzied laughter, said, "Oh, it's all right, Kensington-Ffoulke, I'll carry your debt. For awhile."

"Pah!" said Kensington-Ffoulke.

At last I had to swallow K's final emission, and then I waited while the three players reached down to their crotches, stuffed themselves into their pants, got up and dispersed, K muttering all the while. Jeremy bade his buddies good night. Then he lifted the cloth, and I crawled from under the table and stood up, my mouth twisted possibly (probably) into a grin bordering on the slightly lunatic. My rising was not graceful, because, to be honest, parts of myself were stuck to other parts of myself.

Jeremy embraced me in a bear hug.

"Tompkins," he giggled into my ear, "how did you do it? All three of them were so rattled that they couldn't stop making mistakes, especially Kensington-Ffoulke, and now each of them owes me money, especially Kensington-Ffoulke. Whatever you did, you were wonderful!"

"Thank you, sir," I responded as he held me at arm's length. "I just...diverted them so that they could not concentrate on the game, and—well, I'm glad you won, sir."

"Oh, so am I," he said ebulliently. "So am I. Why, do you

suppose, didn't they just check to see what was going on...down there?"

"For many reasons, sir. I suppose it was partially because they were experiencing pleasure. A great many men, when they are stimulated, don't ask from whence that stimulation is coming, and they stop thinking when they are experiencing pleasure, and they certainly don't think that they want the pleasure to terminate. I am very good at giving pleasure, and so I think that they did not want me—or whatever they thought was exciting them—to cease. Perhaps they had never had happen to them what happened to them tonight. And I like to think, sir, that I give men a unique experience."

"Ah. Tompkins, you're so much more knowledgeable than me."

"'Than I,' sir. And I know, sir."

As he regarded me, his forehead creased slightly, indicating thought, he said, rather hesitantly, "Tompkins, could you... would you be willing...to show me, uh, whatever you did that was so diverting, so unique?"

I hesitated—momentarily. Whatever I said or did would change quite definitely the relationship between my master and me—between, rather, Jeremy and me.

"Yes, sir," I said.

And I did.

# BRASS RAGS

## J. L. Merrow

S houldn't your man be doing that for you, Algy?"

Lord Algernon Huffingham paused in the act of unpacking his valise. "He should, if I had brought one, but as I didn't, he can't."

"Oh?" Cedric Whyte, known to his friends, inevitably, as "Chalky," lounged back on his elbows on Algy's bed. He kicked his feet idly over the edge. "Want me to lend you my chap?"

"That's kind of you, but no, thank you; I'll manage." Algy had had dealings with Cedric's valet, Woundsworth, before, and the man was a dreadful old stick-in-the-mud. Far easier to endure a spot of manual labor than Woundsworth's sanctimonious expressions. And there was always the possibility Algy might have left something incriminating lurking amongst his collars.

"Well, if you're sure. What's happened to old Hibbert, anyway?"

"Brass rags, I'm afraid."

"Come again?"

Algy straightened, pressing his hands into his aching back. An errant lock of his light-brown hair had fallen over one eye, and he squinted at it reproachfully, wondering if he'd remembered to pack brush and comb. "I had to give him his notice."

"Catch him pawning your watch, did you?"

"Not exactly. But he was taking liberties." Algy sighed and ambled over to the mirror. "Taking time off without so much as a by-your-leave, making free with the best claret, and talking back to me in front of the other servants. It seems to happen with all of them. Just because I like some things…a certain *way*, they start thinking they can get away with murder."

"Sorry, old man, don't follow your drift."

Engaged in making the same discovery as countless young men before him—namely, that fingers make a rather poor substitute for a comb—Algy was annoyed to see his reflected cheeks flush a delicate shade of rose. With his fair hair and blue eyes, it made him look like an impeccably tailored cherub, which was not at *all* the sort of impression he preferred to make. "We were…well, *you know.*"

"Oh. *Oh.*" The frown lines deepened, until Cedric's forehead resembled the surface of the sea on a choppy afternoon around Biscay. "I say, don't you think it's a bit off, buggering the help? I'm sure—"

"Keep your voice down! The last thing I need is anyone *else* I have to pay off." Flying to the door, Algy stuck his head out and glanced left, right and, to be on the safe side, up and down, then retreated, shutting it firmly behind him. "Anyway, if you must know, *he* was buggering me."

"Good Lord. And now he's demanding money with menaces?"

"Insinuations, more like, but that's about the size of it."

"What will you do?"

"Do? Pay him off, of course." Algy sat down heavily on the bed next to his friend. "I really thought he was different, Chalky. Why do they always end up despising me? And you needn't answer that."

"Right-oh," Cedric said obligingly. "You know, you really should find someone, well, a bit more like *us*. Someone who'd have as much to lose."

"Care to suggest a few names?" Algy asked, scathingly.

"Well, there's Portonbury—"

"That would be 'Pox' Portonbury, I presume?"

"Or Caldwell—"

"Please. If 'Sissy' Caldwell's wrists were any limper, he'd be in grave danger of losing his hands. I may as well marry a woman and have done with it."

"Well…"

"Not in a million years. Not if she were as rich as Croesus and a Venus incarnate."

"Oh. Well, there's, ah, Melthorpe—"

"No, it's no use, Chalky. I just don't *like* men like that."

"Like what?"

"Like *us*. I like…well…"

"'Horny-handed sons of toil?'"

"In a word, yes."

"Ah. Well, that's the problem, isn't it? You're lowering yourself to their level, and naturally they won't see you as above them anymore."

"I've no particular problem with that. I just wish they wouldn't see themselves as above *me*, is all."

"Except in the purely physical sense, you mean." Cedric nodded. "Well, frankly, Algy, to coin a phrase, you're buggered."

\* \* \*

Buggered, Algy thought sadly to himself some time later, was the one thing he was not. He kicked moodily at a dandelion— or possibly a rhododendron; horticulture had never been his forte—as he strolled through the rather lovely grounds of Blithering Coombe, Cedric's father's estate. It was a damned shame it hadn't worked out with Hibbert. In many ways, he'd been the ideal servant: discreet, reliable and a stevedore in the sack.

Where on God's green earth was Algy going to find another man like that?

As so often when his thoughts turned to potential lovers, Algy found his feet had turned toward the stables. There were so many interesting things to be found there—whips, bridles, assorted arcane items of leather and brass, their purpose lost in the mists of time. Algy adjusted himself hastily in his trousers. Oh, he'd spent many a happy hour in his father's stables, his face in the hay and his arse in the air, his nostrils filled with the sweet aroma of horseshit while his favorite groom beat him black and blue. Once the man had even put a saddle on him and ridden him around the yard, Algy fondly recalled.

It hadn't lasted, of course. Father had banned him from going within fifty yards of the stables back at Fetheram Hoo, claiming the horses were starting to suffer from neglect. Still, Algy thought, brightening a little, Sir William, Cedric's father, had put in place no such prohibition. And a little nostalgic visit would do no one any harm.

Smiling happily, Algy quickened his pace until he reached his destination, whereupon he darted a quick glance around, then slipped inside—and almost walked straight into a pair of firm, hairy buttocks, which tensed and flexed as Algy watched them. Attached to the buttocks, Algy could see a fine pair of shapely, muscular legs, round the ankles of which pooled livery trousers.

It was one of the footmen, he surmised. The rest of the man was in keeping with the general theme: a broad, well-sculpted back, sturdy neck, and dark hair, the natural unruliness of which had entirely failed to be restrained by its coating of brilliantine.

Algy's mouth was suddenly as dry as the fresh hay piled by the door. Beneath the footman, he could discern the form of another, slighter man, fetchingly draped over a low bench strewn with various articles of tack. What little of the smaller man that was visible—mostly, a pair of rather skinny, yet unmistakably masculine legs—twitched and writhed as the footman pounded into him, his harsh breathing a piquant counterpoint to the sweet tune of the slap of bollocks on buttocks.

Terrified, lest a whimper escape him and halt this arousing display, Algy shoved a hand into his mouth as far as it would go. Meanwhile, his other hand, having a pretty fair idea of what was expected of it in such circumstances, had shoved itself down the front of his trousers—not, perhaps, as far as it would go, but certainly to very useful effect.

The grunts from the two lusty young men before him intensified, as did the delicious sensations in Algy's nethers. Recollecting in time that he had, at present, no valet to remove any stains that might occur, Algy thought it prudent to unbutton his trousers. Thus freed from all restrictions, his hand worked more forcefully upon his prick, unconsciously falling into step with the rhythm of the men in front of him. Lord, what wouldn't Algy give to be the object of the footman's attentions! His arse clenched forlornly, feeling empty and bereft, but his cock, God, his cock was on fire and his balls were about to explode.

Sweat dripped down Algy's face as he pumped away, one dribble reaching his lips, which he dreamily licked at. The intense salty flavor was like a shot of brandy. The footman's rhythm was becoming ragged. He had to be close to completion.

Lord, if Algy could only time this right…Yes! YES! The footman groaned and gave a powerful thrust, just as Algy convulsed, his seed spurting out fully six feet across the hay and falling only inches short of the footman's behind.

As the footman collapsed with an oath across his companion's back, Algy came to himself, helped by a sharp pain in his left hand which reminded him he was in the process of biting off several knuckles. Bother. Hopefully, the teeth marks would fade before he needed to appear in company. If not, he would just have to invent some encounter with a wild beast, which was not, after all, all that far from the truth.

Algy gave his injured hand a quick shake and then adjusted himself, checked for any visible stains and slipped out quietly. It was probably time to dress for dinner.

Having laboriously donned white tie and tails entirely unaided, Algy gave himself a pat on the back for a job well done, checked his reflection one last time and sauntered out of his room in search of cocktails. He had barely set foot upon the staircase when something of a commotion in the hall below arrested his attention.

Algy stopped and stared. One of the footmen was being frog-marched across the hall by his fellow footman and the butler. The captive was the attractive one from the stables, Algy realized. If the unruly dark curls hadn't told him this, the wisps of hay adhering to his trousers certainly would have. Algy *tutted* at such carelessness before glancing down hastily at his own lower garments for any similar betraying signs. Then he recollected he'd just changed the blasted things for dinner.

The footman's dark features were even darker now, and his expression was a mixture of pain—for his arms were twisted behind his back—and bravado. He was expostulating with his captors both loudly and profanely, and Algy felt his loins stir in entirely inappropriate fashion. But, by God, the fellow looked magnificent!

Sir William burst out of his dressing room with a face like thunder, his collar only half-fastened. "What is the meaning of all this?" he bellowed downstairs, nearly deafening Algy, who had the misfortune to be only three feet away.

The butler, Franklin, was quick to answer. "It's Robert, sir. The second footman. He's been caught stealing."

Sir William looked sternly at the unhappy fellow. "Well?" he said sharply. "What do you say to these accusations?"

"I only took what was owed me, Sir William." Robert was a picture of righteous indignation, only slightly marred by his ever-shifting gaze.

"Explain, Franklin." Sir William descended, his heavy tread upon the stairs queasily akin, in Algy's ears, to the drumbeat that precedes an execution.

Franklin sniffed. "I found the man helping himself from the petty cash, which I had taken out to pay the grocer's boy and not yet returned to the safe."

Robert snarled at him. "That was my money, that was!" He turned to his employer. "This bastard—begging your pardon, sir—said he was goin' to dock my wages for somefin' I ain't never broke. So I was just getting my money back." His accent, Algy noted with a little frisson, had shifted entirely from drawing room to Whitechapel.

"Is this true, Franklin?"

The butler sniffed again. Algy was on the point of offering him a handkerchief. "All of the servants are quite aware that if they break something, they must pay for it. And there was no one else in the room when Lady Emily entered and found her favorite vase in pieces upon the hearth."

Sir William nodded. "Well then, you've done your duty, Franklin. Get him out of my sight and call the constable." He turned away, the matter closed. Robert's chin remained up, defiant to the last, but there was a sort of hopeless tension about his eyes that wrung the heart.

Algy found himself flying down the stairs with barely a conscious thought. "I say," he said, breathlessly. "Awfully sorry—ought to have said something before—but it was I who broke the thing. Afraid it slipped my mind. I shall be glad to pay for it, of course."

Franklin glared at him. To Algy's surprise, so did the prisoner.

Sir William, being constrained by the rules of politeness, merely harrumphed. "I see. Well, I suppose the fellow had some genuine sense of grievance. Very well then. Franklin, no need to involve the police."

"But Sir William, common thievery—"

"He's dismissed, Franklin, without a character. I think that will suffice. Now, if you will all excuse me, I should like to return to my guests." He turned on his heel and left the hall.

Franklin and the footman reluctantly let go of their prize, who shook his arms like the apostles shaking the dust off their feet, only with rather more in the way of muttered curses than Algy would have attributed to the saints. While the other two departed, Robert stood there, still glaring at Algy. "Well, thanks a bleedin' bundle," he said, sourly, once they were alone.

Algy blinked. "I beg your pardon? I just saved you from gaol you ungrateful wretch!"

Robert snorted. "Ha! It's your fault I'm out a place, though, ain't it? If you 'adn't of gorn and broke that bleedin' vase..."

Too late, Algy realized that to admit that his confession had been fabricated would be to give away more than would be entirely prudent. The former footman had a demonstrably elastic grasp on morals; to explain that Algy had admired his arse while watching him bugger the stable lad and had experienced a reluctance to see said arse languish in gaol would be tantamount to signing a blank check for the fellow. "Oh. Yes, I can see you might not view my actions in a completely favorable light."

"Well, it ain't like the old bugger's going to give me a reference, now is it? So how'm I going to find another place?"

"As it happens, I'm in need of a valet," Algy suggested cautiously. "Do you think you could turn your hand to that sort of work?"

Robert regarded him for a moment, rather in the manner of one considering the purchase of a prize thoroughbred. Algy half expected a demand that he show his teeth. "All right. I'll be your valet, and, at the end of it, you give me a reference, right?" His eyes narrowed. "A *good* reference."

"A sterling reference," Algy assured him. "I shall extol your virtues in terms that would make the Bard of Avon blush."

Those handsome brown eyes became the merest slits. "Right. So are we staying 'ere long? 'Cos Franklin's going to be at me to sling me 'ook."

"Sling *my* hook," Algy corrected absentmindedly. "Well, I suppose in the circumstances it might be politic to remove ourselves. Very well. I'll go and explain matters to Cedric, have them bring the Wolseley around and then we'll be off. We can stop for dinner at a pub en route. You go and pack your things." He smiled as a pleasant thought struck him. "And then you can pack mine."

Three days after they had arrived back at Algy's Mayfair town house, however, he was feeling rather less chipper. Robert had proved himself, if not a particularly satisfactory valet at present, certainly an admirably quick learner. That was part of the trouble.

Close proximity to Robert had only served to amplify his roguish charms in Algy's eyes, and Algy had been struck with an attack of wholly unwonted—and heartily unwanted—nerves. Whilst the man had proved himself an able student in the matter of pressing shirts, there had been absolutely no progress toward the matter closest to Algy's heart. (In metaphorical terms, that is. In purely physical terms it was a good eighteen inches away. Lessening to ten, obviously, when aroused.)

Algy had found himself, uncharacteristically, shying away from the object of his desire. He didn't just wish Robert to indulge his carnal impulses; Algy wanted the man to think *well* of him, to admire him, if at all possible, at least to some degree as much as Algy admired Robert. It was both mortifying and frustrating in equal measure.

And it wasn't as though there hadn't been any amount of opportunity for Algy to press his suit. Or press anything else, for that matter. From his schooldays, Algy had been well-versed in the art of lingering touches, and, for heaven's sake, Robert assisted him to disrobe on a daily basis. But Algy, sadly, found himself paralyzed at such times.

Take the matter of the bath yesterday—a perfect opportunity, Algy knew. All it usually took was a simple invitation to scrub the master's back, which would progress into a plea for help in cleansing all those difficult-to-reach nooks and crevices. Then the flicking of damp towels could begin in earnest.

Robert had drawn the bath and stood respectfully by, a towel over one arm like a well-dressed railing. While he awaited Algy's pleasure, the man had made some innocuous comment on the linoleum in the bathroom. Algy had been occupied, at the time, with examining his reflection—had that been a gray hair? Surely not—and had answered somewhat distractedly, "Yes, I find it's easier on the knees."

Something about the sudden stillness in the steam-filled air had led him to look up at Robert, who was now staring at him a trifle oddly.

It was the moment, Algy realized, to declare himself. To lay his cards—and, if successful, himself—upon the table. Or, of course, any other convenient surface. Algy gathered up his courage. Unfortunately, his courage gathered up its skirts and ran, mewling, for the door. "Ah," he said quickly. "I mean, for the scrubber." Mortified, he entertained brief thoughts of diving headfirst into his bath and drowning himself. "That is, the person whose job it is to, well…"

"Scrub?"

"Yes. Exactly. I wouldn't want you to think I'm in the habit of consorting with low women."

Robert regarded him, an unreadable expression on his face. "My old ma was a scrubber," he finally said.

"Oh?"

"'Course, that was in her younger days. Cleanest doorstep on the street, we 'ad."

"That's…good. Very good. Carry on, Robert." Algy fled, quite forgetting he'd intended to take a bath.

As matters stood, Algy was genuinely glad when Robert announced the arrival of his friend Cedric. Old Chalky was always good for a distraction from one's own abject failure in whatever endeavor, Algy had found. Many had been the time in their mutual schooldays when Algy had sought solace in his friend's company after an unsuccessful midnight raid on the kitchens or, as might be, the groundsman's bedroom.

Robert served drinks, then stood respectfully by the wall awaiting orders—and eavesdropping shamelessly, of course, but Algy could hardly begrudge the fellow that.

"So what brings you here, old chum? Life at Blithering too deathly dull without me?"

"No, actually it's this business about Robert. I've been feeling terrible about the whole thing. You see, it was I who broke that blasted vase. I was smoking a quick cigarillo before dinner and I found myself without an ashtray. So I thought, finally, this hideous old thing of Mother's can be of some use. Unfortunately, I was a little less than careful while tapping off the old ash, and before I knew it, there was an almighty crash and a hearth full of antique Chinese smithereens."

Algy regarded his old friend with eyebrows raised. "And it never occurred to you to just tap your ash into the fireplace?"

Cedric frowned. "I'd have had to crouch down to do that, or it would have gone everywhere in the draught from the flue. Either way, my trousers would have been ruined. You know what Woundsworth is like when I sully my clothes. Gives me that look, as though I'm far too dim to be allowed out in public."

"I can't imagine where he gets that idea."

"Neither can I! Anyway, long story short, no sooner had I realized what had happened than the door opened. Of course, I wasn't going to stick around to get the blame. Mother would have sent me to bed without any supper, as likely as not, and we were having pheasant. You know how I adore pheasant, especially with redcurrant jelly—"

"I thought you said this was the *short* version?" Algy tapped his fingers.

"Don't interrupt, Algy. Now I've forgotten where I was."

"Running away from the scene of the crime."

"Oh! Yes. Well, I didn't really have time to run. So I simply ducked behind the sofa. And, well, you know the rest. Poor old Robert got the blame, and I was just going to slip him the money on the q.t., plus a little extra, of course, but he, ah, went and took matters into his own hands."

Algy experienced a somewhat light-headed moment at the thought of Robert taking matters into his own hands, but forced himself to concentrate. "And now?"

"Well, I had to come clean, of course. There was a fearful row. But anyway, I've persuaded Father that Robert should have his job back." Cedric leaned back in his chair and beamed at them happily.

Robert's expression gave no hint of his feelings. "That's very kind of you, sir."

"Hang about." Algy frowned. There might have been the suspicion of a pout in there, too. "The man's my valet now. You can't go stealing him from me. You had him and you lost him, and now he's mine. Finders keepers."

Cedric's brow furrowed. "But you know he hasn't been trained as a valet. Wouldn't you rather have someone experienced?"

"Robert is *quite* experienced enough for me," Algy snapped, thinking back to that scene in the stables, and the sight of firm, muscular buttocks pumping away forcefully, while Algy's hand did its best to ape the rhythm. "What's the matter with you?" he demanded, coming back to himself, only to realize that Cedric had gone a little pink.

"Oh. Ah. Fine, old chap. I hadn't realized you and Robert were—"

"*Pas devant les domestiques!*"

The furrows deepened. "Algy? Why are you speaking Greek? You know I was always terrible at that sort of thing at school."

Algy sank his head into his hands and groaned.

"Anyway, if that's the way it is," Cedric carried on briskly, "of course I shouldn't dream of insisting on having him back. Although I must say, you don't hang around, do you? You must have barely had time to have the linen laundered since old Hibbert hopped out of bed."

Algy sighed and resolutely did not *look* at Robert. "Chalky, would you mind awfully taking a walk, on your own? A nice long one would be good. I should like to consult with my manservant."

Cedric nodded. "Oh, absolutely. You 'consult' away." He tapped his finger to the side of his nose. "Mum's the word. I'll be at my club."

Once Cedric had ambled out of the door, Algy glared at Robert. "Well, you've been pretty quiet."

"Didn't think it was my place to say nothing, my Lord."

"*Anything*. Not 'nothing.' And yes, of course it was your place. *Your place* was what we were bloody well talking about."

"Yes, my Lord." He paused. "What I don't understand is, if it wasn't you what broke that vase—he's right, you know, ugly as sin that 'orrible thing was—why'd you say it was? You didn't owe me nothing—um, *anything*—my Lord."

"I don't suppose you'd believe I'm just a naturally kind-hearted person? No, don't answer that. Look, if you want to go back to Blithering, if you've got someone you're missing back there…" Algy girded himself to bite the bullet. "Dash it all, I saw you in the stables. With—actually, I have no idea who you were with. One of the grooms, I suppose. He had rather delicate ankles—anyway, the point is, if you want to get back to him, I shan't stand in your way. But otherwise, well, I was hoping perhaps we might come to some sort of arrangement. If the idea is agreeable to you."

Robert's face was guarded. "And *exactly* what sort of

arrangement might that be?"

Algy shrugged, going for nonchalance but achieving something more akin to a nervous tic. "Well, you are a fellow who enjoys the company of other fellows, and, as it happens, so am I. It seems to me it might be to our mutual advantage were we to, shall we say, cut out the middle man?"

Robert frowned. "I don't want nuffin' to do with no freesomes."

"Threesomes. With a *th*. And it's *nothing*. No-thing. And who on earth mentioned threesomes? I was intending to keep this strictly between ourselves."

Robert pursed his lips in a speculative fashion. Then he nodded. "That'd be all right, then."

"Really? You'd be, *ahem*, interested?"

"From what I've seen, you've been 'iding a pair of pretty delicate ankles yourself under them posh wool trousers." Robert gave a roguish wink.

Algy felt all hot and fluttery inside. "I should warn you, I have certain...unusual tastes," he confessed.

"Yeah?"

"I, ah, appreciate a firm hand. Within the context of said arrangement."

"'Ooze?"

"What?"

"'Ooze 'and?"

"I—oh. W*h*ose *h*and. That would be, ah, yours." He swallowed. "And I might, let us say, encourage a certain informality of speech that wouldn't be appropriate in public. Say, for instance, you wished to, ah, chastise me. Verbally, I mean. Although the other sort would do quite admirably, too. Would any of that be, ah, objectionable to you?" Algy was quite certain his face was redder than a beetroot.

"Sounds all right to me, my Lord. Tell yer what, d'you want me to get yer bath ready?" Robert smirked. "Help your lordship get 'is clothes off, that sort of fing? I mean, *thing.*"

He was a man of action. Algy rather thought he might be in love. "Excellent idea. Although perhaps it would be as well to run downstairs first and let the rest of the servants know they have the afternoon off."

Robert laughed. "Bloody 'ell. I was wondering what Cook was on about. She was complaining only this morning they 'adn't 'ad no afternoons off since I got 'ere, and why didn't I do something about it?"

Algy shrugged a little awkwardly. "One's servants do rather accustom themselves to one's ways."

A short while later, the house was empty and silent, save for the sound of Algy's pounding heart, which he was certain would have the neighbors round to complain any moment. Robert had a roguish glint in his eye as he entered the bathroom, where Algy awaited him, and shut the door. "So what 'appens now, my Lord?"

Algy swallowed. "Now we take off our clothes. All of them, if you wouldn't mind. I only saw one side of you back at Blithering."

"Yeah, but it was me best side." Robert grinned and slapped his own arse. Algy had to close his eyes briefly at the sight and, Lord, the sound. When he opened them again, Robert was standing there naked in front of him.

"Good God, man, you're stupendous," he gasped, mesmerized by Robert's broad, well-furred chest, his flat stomach and, most importantly, the way his cock swelled and rose under Algy's appreciative gaze. It soon stood bolt upright, and both length and girth put Algy irresistibly in mind of the old chestnut trees at Fetheringham Hoo. He'd seen one of them being felled as a boy, and it struck him that had its fall been filmed using one of those motion picture cameras the French were so fond of, and had the film of that fall been played backward, it would have looked uncannily like the majestic rise to tumescence of Robert's manhood.

As a lad, running about his father's estate, Algy had always enjoyed watching the gardeners fell trees. There was just something about a man pounding away rhythmically, the sweat on his shirtless torso gleaming in the sunlight and both hands upon his mighty chopper...

Robert's voice cut into Algy's reverie like a butter-knife that had been dipped in honey. Algy couldn't wait to become the muffin for that knife. "Want me to 'elp you undress, my Lord?"

"That, ah, that might be wise." Algy was positive he'd had the use of his fingers this morning when he woke up, but they appeared now to be so many nerveless sausages affixed to his hands by some jovial butcher.

Robert's fingers, by contrast, were nimble creatures, darting across Algy's body to swift effect. Algy found himself entirely distracted from their progress by Robert's proximity. His naked flesh seemed to radiate heat in Algy's direction, and his scent was a heady mix of brilliantine, carbolic soap and cheap tobacco. Algy would have to do something about that, he decided deliriously—make the man a present of a box of French cigarettes or some such thing.

Soon Algy's shirt and trousers were a neat pile upon a chair, his silk undergarments swift to follow. Algy stood in the bathroom as naked as the day he was born, although, he hoped, rather more physically appealing than he had been back then. Robert was giving him a frank appraisal that had Algy's cock sitting up and begging. Which, come to think of it, was exactly what the rest of him wanted to be doing right about then.

Algy's knees seemed to give way without any need for instruction, dropping him to the floor and allowing him to nuzzle happily into the base of Robert's mighty Doric column. The scent of musk and honest, manly sweat suffused Algy's nostrils, and Robert's balls tightened pleasingly under his ministrations. "Tell me what to do," Algy pleaded.

Robert pulled away slightly. "'Ang about, I fort you'd done this before."

Algy rolled his eyes. "*Obviously* I've done this before. Firm hand, remember?"

"Oh. Right." There was a short silence, then a sudden intake of breath. "Orl right. Suck it, then. You 'eard me. Get your mouth on my prick."

Algy's eyes fell shut in heady pleasure as Robert's prodigious erection plunged between his lips. The salty flavor was like ambrosia on his tongue, and even the gagging produced by an overenthusiastic thrust was familiar and welcome, like an old school chum turning up unexpectedly for dinner.

"That's right," Robert was saying. "Suck it hard. Go on. You can take it." Algy's cock twitched happily between his legs.

When he judged that Robert was in danger of losing control, Algy pulled back.

"Oi! I never said stop," Robert grumbled, but his gaze was alert, waiting for Algy's cues.

"I'm sorry," Algy said abjectly. His heart pounded. This was all going so well, and he might just be about to ruin it utterly, but, Lord, it could be *perfect*, if Robert wasn't about to turn from him in disgust. "But I need, well, that is, if you wouldn't mind...obviously, if you'd rather not, we can...but I really would be most awfully grateful if you'd..."

Robert rolled his eyes. "Bloody 'ell, just spit it out. 'Ow bad can it be?"

Algy groaned. "Piss on me."

"Come again?"

"I said, piss on me. On my head."

"Bloody 'ell, you don't ask much, do you? Gimme 'arf a mo."
Relief flooded through Algy as Robert turned away, most definitely not in disgust if the stiffness of the man's cock was any
judge. The faint sound of times-tables being recited reached
Algy's ears as he waited, head bent, the bathroom linoleum
beginning to stick to his knees.

"Fifty-six," Algy interjected helpfully.

"Wot?"

"Seven eights are fifty-six. Not fifty-four."

"Oh, buggering 'ell...tell yer what, though, that's done the
trick. Here we go."

Algy groaned again as the hot stream hit him. The first salvo
went awry, striking his shoulder, but Robert adjusted his aim
and soon that rich, golden torrent was soaking Algy's hair and
running in rivulets down his face.

"Look at me," Robert snarled, obviously getting into his
role. And, with a whimper, Algy looked up. Robert's prodigious
fountain of piss struck him full in the face, getting in his nose,
his ears, and his eyes where it stung like the dickens. It was
heaven. "That's it," Robert growled, shaking the last few drops
off his prick. "Er, now what?" he asked, uncertainly.

Algy rolled his stinging eyes. "Make me clean it up!"

Robert nodded. Obviously that made sense to him. *Finally.*
"Orl right, get that shirt and wipe up this mess you've made."

Algy scrambled to obey, mopping up the puddles on the lino
with Jermyn Street's finest. As he worked, more drips fell from
his sodden hair, elevating his task to Sisyphean status.

"That'll do," Robert grunted after a goodly while.
"Now..."

"Punishment!" Algy cued him.

"Right. I want your head on the floor and yer arse in the air."

Algy did as he was bid, almost panting in his eagerness. "Did I say put yer 'ands behind yer back? Put 'em on the floor. I don't want you touching me with your filthy mitts." He waited while Algy complied. "Now, what sorta punishment d'you think you deserve for making such a filthy mess?"

Appreciating Robert's finesse in staying in character while asking instructions, Algy waggled his arse a little. "Spanking," he groaned.

"What was that? Speak up, *your Whoreship*, I din't 'ear you!"

At Robert's roar, Algy whimpered, mortally afraid he was going to come before he was even touched. "Spank me! Spank me hard! I'm a filthy, dirty whore and I ought to be spanked!"

There was an agonizing pause—then a far more exquisitely agonizing *thwack*—as Robert's hand met Algy's buttock. Algy yelped.

"You all right, my Lord?"

"Yes! Spank me harder! I'm a trollop, a whore—give it all you've got, man!"

Algy was rather certain he could hear a muttered "Bloody 'ell!" but it was only moments before that thick, meaty hand came down on his tender arse, again and again. Algy whimpered with each strike, skinning his knees as he skidded forward on the linoleum with the force of the blows. His buttocks were on fire, and his mind was as well. He couldn't remember the last time anyone had hit him so hard, and his balls felt like they were about to burst. "Please!" he sobbed, the onslaught ceasing.

"Please what?" came in cautious tones.

"Please bugger me!"

"*Finally*," Robert breathed, and Algy heard the sound of

spitting, then felt huge gobbets of saliva worked into his crack. And then it was the turn of a huge cockhead, which stretched him mercilessly, forcing its way in.

Algy's breath came in thick sobs as that massive manhood invaded his insides. "Yes, more, yes..." he babbled, vaguely conscious of swearing coming from behind him. "Use me, plough me, take me like the filthy little sodomite I am..." And then, heaven of heavens, Robert changed the angle and started to batter at his prostate, and then, oh Lord, there was the massive sting of a strong hand striking his already sore buttock, and Algy was sobbing and coming, pulsing out his soul onto the linoleum. He was barely aware of Robert's continued thrusting, finally coming to full consciousness of his surroundings as Robert stilled and shuddered, filling him up with his seed.

"Fuckin' 'ell," Robert breathed, collapsing on Algy in a not-altogether-comfortable way. "You little fucking pervert. My Lord."

Despite being squashed and aching all over from a myriad little (and not-so-little) hurts, Algy was floating on an ocean of happiness. "Bloody right," he murmured. "Robert, you were marvelous."

"Thank you, my Lord."

"Don't mention it." Algy attempted to shift himself from the now decidedly grubby bathroom floor. "Ah, do you think you could get off me? Thank you."

"Would you like me to run you that bath now, my Lord?"

"That would be splendid."

A short while later, Algy lay back in a sea of warm bubbles and warmer contentment. That had gone rather well, he mused. What Robert lacked in experience with Algy's particular predilections, he certainly made up for in enthusiasm.

Yes, Algy thought, closing his eyes in bliss. This was all

going to work out splendidly. Next time, he daydreamed, he'd introduce Robert to the contents of his old school trunk. Old Hibbert had been such a namby-pamby with the whip. Algy had a feeling Robert would have no such qualms.

Robert was thoughtful as he put the kettle on for tea. That'd been an education, and no mistake. Who'd have thought a toff like his Lordship would get off on being handled like a tuppenny-ha'penny whore? Still, it took all sorts, that's what his old ma always said, and she ought to know, seeing as how she'd done her time on the streets before she'd met his step-dad and gone respectable.

Well, Robert was in gravy here, no two ways about it. Archie in the stables had been all right for a tumble, but he didn't hold a candle to a man like his Lordship. Lord Algernon was handsome, clever and kind, and he wanted Robert to better himself, and as Ma always said, them's the ones to hold on to. *And* he had much better ankles than Archie. No, if Lord Algy wanted to be treated like a Piccadilly renter, Robert was more than happy to oblige. Next time, Robert reckoned, he'd get out his Lordship's riding crop and show him something else he'd learned in the stables.

When the kettle began to whistle, Robert whistled right along with it.

# MUTABLE
# MEMORIES

## Michael Bracken

At the turn of the century, I worked for Michael Fairchild, a confirmed bachelor living off of inherited money. In 1900, the day after Christmas, he sent me from the city by train to open up the Connecticut house, to stock the kitchen and bar, and to prepare for the year-end celebration, when he would host several dozen of his equally spoiled friends in a night of drunken debauchery in order to welcome the twentieth century.

The housekeeper—an elderly woman who lived with her groundskeeper husband in a cottage on the eastern edge of the property—helped remove and store the sheets that covered and protected the furniture several months of each year. She also gave the entire house a thorough cleaning in preparation for guests, while her husband tidied up the grounds following a Christmas Day storm that scattered several broken branches across the lawn. The entire estate—a furnished eight-bedroom home, several outbuildings that included a water tower to gravity-feed the indoor plumbing, and the elderly couple who cared for it all—had been inherited from Fairchild's grandfather when the old man died during a visit to a bathhouse in the city. Much of the hard liquor that would be served during the celebration traveled with me by train, and Fairchild's cook, a stout woman who brooked no dissent, gave me a long list of foodstuffs to acquire locally prior to her arrival the Sunday before the grand affair. As per my instructions, I ensured that all was in order when my employer arrived midmorning New Year's Eve. I stood waiting on the porch as soon as I heard his horseless carriage sputtering up the long drive.

Fairchild brought the foul-smelling thing to a halt at the bottom of the steps and climbed out. He peeled off his cloth peaked cap and driving goggles as he bounded up the steps. When I met him halfway, he shoved them into my hands, peeled off his gloves, and quickly unbuttoned his leather storm coat, adding them to my burden. "Get my bags and take them to my room, Stevens. I need to bathe and change clothes before the guests arrive."

I had a first name, but Fairchild never used it. I replied, "Yes, sir. Right away, sir."

My employer had disappeared into the house by then and I doubt if he heard my response. I shifted my load of discarded driving clothes and grabbed both the valise and the suit bag from the passenger seat of his horseless carriage. Then I followed him inside, past the grandfather clock in the foyer, and carried everything up the stairs to the master bedroom at the far end of the hall. I then hung his storm coat in the wardrobe along with most of the contents of the suit bag and unpacked the valise before putting its contents in the dresser. When I finished, I returned to the main floor and found the housekeeper in a tizzy, as Fairchild had tracked something greasy across the hardwood floor.

After listening to her laud Fairchild's grandfather for his obsessive fastidiousness, and after assuring her that Fairchild would return to the city by week's end, I went in search of her husband.

In the city, people would gather at City Hall Park that night to hear John Philip Sousa's band perform while they watched the century count down on the big clock, but Fairchild had other plans. He had me hire a quintet of musicians from the city to perform lively dance music, and I sent the groundskeeper to the train station to greet their arrival and transport them back to the house.

Once Fairchild was satisfied with the liquor selection, that the cook had things well under control in the kitchen, and that the musicians would soon arrive, I followed him upstairs. While I drew his bath, he stripped off the clothes he'd worn during his drive from the city and tossed them in a heap for me to care for later.

Though he had yet to go to fat, as he would later in life, Fairchild had the physique of a man who had never lifted a finger in hard labor. Blue eyed, sandy haired, clean shaven, pale of skin and with little body hair save for the nest cradling his cock and balls, he reminded me of a man much younger than his years. I felt my cock stir at the sight of his nudity just as it had the first time I'd seen him in the bathhouse and nearly every time since.

"How do I look, Stevens?"

I wet my lips with the tip of my tongue and replied, "Delicious."

My employer smiled and then stepped into the bath. After I scrubbed his back, I left him to finish bathing alone while I laid out his clothing for the evening: a dark blue lounge coat with matching trousers that were cuffed and creased, a white shirt, a dark tie, and two-toned spectators.

I had been with Fairchild since shortly after his grandfather's death, and I attended to his every need, from delivering his breakfast in bed to organizing the orgiastic parties he hosted. He had no particular skill with numbers, leaving me in charge of all of his household accounts. Suffice it to say, with his predilections, Fairchild was unlikely to ever produce an heir, and so, with no incentive to safeguard his grandfather's fortune, he spared no expense in his efforts to impress and outspend the wealthy young malingerers with whom he fraternized.

He walked naked into the master bedroom, a towel in one hand. I took it from him and vigorously dried his back, his buttocks, and the nest of his pubic hair, causing his balls to tighten and his cock to stir.

Fairchild pushed the towel away. "Save it for later," he told me. "Guests should be here any moment."

I helped my employer dress and then followed him downstairs to the living room, where I prepared his first drink of the evening. He'd barely finished it before the first guest arrived, a longtime friend of Fairchild's named Winston Carnegie.

All of Fairchild's guests arrived, just as he had earlier, in horseless carriages, parking the damnable things willy-nilly on the lawn. This gave the groundskeeper apoplectic fits until I convinced him and his wife to return to their cottage and ignore what was happening at the house, and I spent much of the early evening greeting young men at the front door and attending to their driving clothes. Once I felt certain everyone had arrived, I moved about the house, refreshing drinks, collecting empty plates, and appreciating the youthful exuberance of nearly three-dozen young men who valued hedonism above all else and who financed their excesses with the blood and sweat of previous generations.

With pendent lights ablaze in every room, lighting the house up like a Broadway theater, I was able to examine each of the guests in turn. The young men were mostly clean shaven, though a few sported moustaches or sideburns. All had hair cut short in the fashion of the day and were dressed much the same as Fairchild. They were of various heights and weights and body shapes, but all shared the pale skin of carefree men who spent far more time in the dark than in the light.

When these men weren't eating, drinking, smoking and dancing, they were talking. They debated the issues of the day and they laughed about Mark Twain's "A Greeting from the 19th Century to the 20th Century," published in the *New York Herald* the previous day, and about the predictions of the future published in the *New York World*'s supplement "New York as It Will Be in 1999," also published that Sunday. Did anyone really believe that the city would someday be filled with elevated sidewalks that connected skyscrapers with flat roofs designed for airship landings?

As midnight approached, the guests began to pair off, disappearing into one of the seven guest bedrooms and returning to the party a bit later with disheveled clothing and satiated grins. After alcohol diminished their inhibitions and lowered the social barrier between the spoiled wealthy and the help who attended to their needs, I was propositioned half a dozen times and repeatedly had my ass pinched and my crotch fondled. I smiled through it all, knowing full well that my reward would come later.

After I replaced Winston Carnegie's drink for the second time, he grabbed my arm and said, "You're a godsend, Stevens. How did Michael ever find you?"

"Fate," I replied without elaboration.

After an anomaly in household accounting that a previous

employer attributed to my negligence cost me my position, I had been forced to take part-time employment as a towel boy in the bathhouse where I first encountered Fairchild and his grandfather. Invisible to them, I was able to observe their dynamic each time they visited. The allowance Fairchild's grandfather provided wasn't sufficient to maintain the lifestyle Fairchild desired, and the friction between them led to a fatal confrontation.

"Fate?" Carnegie repeated. "I wish fate had dropped you on my doorstep. I'm stuck with a stuffy old codger who's been with the family since my father was a gleam in his father's eye."

"I'm certain your man is quite proficient at his job, sir."

"Oh, Alistair's good enough, but he isn't you," Carnegie said with a wink. "I could have fun with you."

"You still might," I retorted, returning his wink, because I was at all times courteous and accommodating to my employer's friends.

The musicians kept a watchful eye on the clock, silencing the music for a few minutes shortly before midnight. Fairchild led his guests into the foyer for the countdown to the new century, and everyone let out a cheer when the grandfather clock struck the twelfth chime. Then the band played and the guests sang "Auld Lang Syne" while I opened several bottles of champagne.

Discretion disappeared once the new century began. Jackets came off, ties were loosened and before long I found one of the guests giving hand jobs to two other guests in the sitting room. Moments later I found a slender brunet bent over the dining room table while a thick-dicked young blond rogered him in the ass.

Of course, I couldn't help myself. Seeing all the naked male flesh—young and seemingly unaffected by the mass quantities of alcohol consumed throughout the evening—made my cock tent the front of my trousers.

Before she had a chance to witness any of the debauchery, I sent the cook out the back door and across the estate grounds to spend the night with the groundskeeper and the housekeeper. I considered dismissing the band as well, but had nowhere to send them at that time of night, and so they continued playing as if nothing unusual was happening around them.

Another trip through the house, switching off some of the pendant lights as I went, brought me back to the foyer, where I found my employer sitting on the staircase, his trousers around his ankles and his cock in the mouth of an unfamiliar blond. Fairchild held an empty whiskey glass in one hand and had the other hand resting on the back of the fellating young man's bobbing head.

"Stevens!" my employer called when he spotted me watching. He held up the empty glass. "Refill this."

"Yes, sir," I said as I took the glass.

Once his hand was empty, Fairchild pressed it against the back of the blond's head and began bucking his hips up and down, face-fucking the young man.

I'd stepped behind the bar in the living room before my employer came, so I didn't see him ejaculate in the blond's mouth, but I certainly heard him shout the name of a popular deity when he did.

When I returned with Fairchild's whiskey, the blond was nowhere to be seen, nor were my employer's trousers and spectators. Fairchild wore his jacket, shirt and loosened tie, but nothing below that save for his stockings and garters. His saliva-and-come-covered cock was stuck to his thigh, and he unstuck it before standing. He took the drink from my outstretched hand and asked, "Things are going rather well, don't you think, Stevens?"

"Quite well, Mr. Fairchild."

Two naked young men came running from the library, their erections preceding them, and headed up the stairs. Fairchild's gaze followed them. "I think I ought to find out what that's all about."

"Yes, sir."

After my employer also headed up the stairs, I continued patrolling the house, turning off pendent lights as I went. Once most of the downstairs was dark as the night outside, I led the musicians into the kitchen.

A few minutes later, Carnegie found me standing with the band as they wolfed down leftover food. He placed one hand on my back and leaned close to whisper in my ear. "Everyone else has gone upstairs."

"Yes, sir?"

He whispered, "I still think I can have fun with you, Stevens. You're more of a man than any of the boys here tonight."

I certainly was older than Fairchild or any of his guests. "There's only one way to find out, Mr. Carnegie."

He smiled.

I told the band they could sleep on the living room floor if they wished, and that someone would see them to the train station in the morning.

Carnegie had a half-empty glass of whiskey in one hand. After I dipped a cloth napkin in greasy roast beef drippings, I took his other hand and led him to my room in the servant's quarters accessible only through the kitchen. As I closed the door behind us, Carnegie took the greasy napkin from my hand and placed it and his whiskey glass on the nightstand. Then he undressed. When he had removed his trousers and underthings, my cock, already half-erect from several hours spent watching naked young men in various stages of flagrante delicto, immediately stood at rapt attention.

My employer's guest finished undressing and he helped me do the same, quickly revealing my turgid erection and the dark pubic hair surrounding it.

"You've been serving us all evening, Stevens," Carnegie said as he dropped to his knees in front of me. "It's about time someone served you."

He wrapped his fist around my cock and held the shaft tight as he took the mushroom cap of my cockhead into his mouth. He licked all the way around, covering it with his saliva, and then he slowly drew in my entire length. As soon as his warm breath tickled my pubic hair, he drew back, catching his teeth on the swollen glans before doing it again.

I wrapped my hand around the back of Carnegie's head and held it as his face moved up and down the length of my stiff shaft, lubricating my cock with so much saliva that it dampened my pubic hair and dripped from my balls. As he fellated me, he grabbed my wet balls with his free hand and used the tip of his finger to stroke the sensitive spot behind them.

He had teased me long enough. I grasped his head more firmly as I thrust the entire length of my cock into his mouth. Then I drew back and did it again, fucking his face hard and fast. Just when I was about to come, he slipped his saliva-slickened finger back just a little bit farther and pressed it against the tight pucker of my asshole, which immediately opened to him.

I came and came hard, firing thick wads of hot come against the back of Carnegie's throat. He swallowed every drop and held my cock in his mouth until it stopped spasming.

He stood, washed down my load with the last of his whiskey, and turned to face me again. He then picked up the greasy napkin and wrapped it around my semi-flaccid cock, quickly bringing it back to life as he slathered it with natural lubricant. After my cock was covered with roast-beef grease, he used the napkin to wipe behind his balls, lubricating his asshole as best he could before he turned and bent over the bed.

I stepped behind him, grabbed his hips and pressed the head of my grease-slickened cock against his tight little hole. As I pressed forward, Carnegie pressed backward, slowly opening to me. Soon I had the entire length of my cock buried in his ass. I drew back until only my cockhead remained inside him before I pushed forward yet again.

Carnegie was soft but not doughy, his pale skin bruising easily as I gripped him and drilled into his ass. I drew back and slammed my hips forward again and again, fucking him hard and fast until I couldn't hold back any longer. Again I came, rapturously filling his ass with a second load of come.

I stood holding him for the longest time, until my cock finally quit throbbing and began to deflate. I then pulled out of him, sat on the side of the bed and watched as he masturbated in front of me.

When he finished, I pulled him into my narrow bed and we fell asleep wrapped tightly around each other—servant and employer's guest—remaining entwined until the cook returned to the house shortly before sunrise, New Year's Day, and woke us with the clanking of pans.

She fed the musicians breakfast before the groundskeeper took them to the train station and, over the next several hours, prepared dozens of eggs, many rashers of bacon and several loaves of toast, while I in turn offered aspirin, coffee, and hair of the dog to the hungover young men who requested it. Carnegie departed first, and the other guests vacated the house in two and threes, just as they had come. By midday all horseless carriages but Fairchild's were gone from the property, much to relief of the groundskeeper. The housekeeper was far less relieved at the disappearance of Fairchild's guests when she saw the condition of the furnishings, especially when she saw all the stains of unknown origin that would require days of effort to eliminate.

I took Fairchild's breakfast to his room after the last of his guests had driven away, and I settled a short-legged tray over his lap so that he could eat in bed.

"They'll not top last night any time soon," he proclaimed. Outlandish parties and over-the-top affairs were a form of competition among Fairchild's social set, and he seemed confident that he had bested the others with his turn-of-the-century orgy.

"I'm not certain many of them will even remember last night, Mr. Fairchild," I said. We both well knew that memories were mutable things. "Their drink set you back a good bit."

With a wave of his hand, my employer dismissed my concern about the evening's expense, much as I knew he would. What he did not know was that I had paid for alcohol I'd not received and the money kicked back from the liquor wholesaler had found its way into one of my private accounts. I'd not done as well with the foodstuffs—limited as I was by the cook's detailed shopping list and the necessity of having to shop in Connecticut rather than in the city, where I had an extensive network of like-minded suppliers—but I still managed to pocket a few dollars thanks to a heavy-thumbed butcher.

I left Fairchild to finish his breakfast alone, wondering as I walked out of his bedroom if the copious amounts of alcohol and the celebratory sex heralding the arrival of the new century had pushed from his memory the one event that had made it all possible.

Though I remained in Fairchild's employ for two more decades and through several dozen more parties, I finally left him in the early 1920s after I had milked hundreds of thousands of dollars from the household accounts and saw that his remaining bank balance could not much longer sustain his lifestyle. Soon after leaving his employ, I headed west to Hollywoodland and the booming film industry, where I thought a man of my ambition, predilections and skills could easily find opportunities.

As I'd imagined would happen, Fairchild burned through the remains of his inheritance long before Black Friday and the Great Depression erased the wealth of his former social circle. The last I heard anything about him, he was trying to explain away an anonymous letter to the police that implicated him in the untimely death of his grandfather a great many years earlier, an event easily misremembered by at least one of the two living witnesses.

I had been the invisible hired help in the bathhouse's steam room, silent witness to the accident that killed Fairchild's grandfather. The two men had been arguing yet again about Fairchild's demand for an increased allowance, and the young man had pushed his grandfather backward. The old man lost his footing on the slick floor and hit his head on the corner of the wooden bench as he fell. I thought Fairchild would call for help, but he hesitated and knelt beside the old man, seemingly checking for vital signs. Once certain that his grandfather was dead, Fairchild slipped out of the steam room only a few steps ahead of me and was found in the communal bath fifteen minutes later when one of the other members found his grandfather's lifeless body.

The police interviewed all of the bathhouse's members but didn't get around to the employees until the following day, after I'd already had time to speak with Fairchild, mention my years of experience running the households of the well-to-do and describe for him the mutability of my memory.

# FRONT DOOR, BACK DOOR

## Logan Zachary

C harles, hurry. Lord Saxon needs you at the front door,"
Mrs. Marsh, the cook, called out from the back door.

Charles set down the wire paddle he'd been using on a dusty
rug and raced into the house. He headed up the servant's staircase and emerged off the library, then hurried through the main
hall to the front entrance.

Lord Saxon was tugging on the bell pull again. He turned as
he heard the footfalls on the marble floor, then released the pull
and moved to the front door entrance. "Charles, where have
you been?" he demanded, but didn't wait for his response. He
pulled the huge wooden front door open and stormed down the
stairs and out to the street.

Charles slowed, then paused, as he neared the front door.
He'd never before passed through it.

"Well, hurry up, boy, before the neighbors see."

Charles raced down the steps and joined his master on the
street.

A huge pile of horse manure steamed in the cold morning air.

Lord Saxon rolled his eyes heavenward. "Where is your bucket and shovel?"

"I...I..." was all Charles could get out of his mouth.

"Clean this mess up now, before the neighbors see it. And hurry up about it!" Lord Saxon clapped his hands and sent Charles scurrying back into the house, down the stairs to the kitchen. Charles then found an ash bucket and shovel and raced back to the front door.

Lord Saxon looked at him in disdain and pointed to the mess.

Charles knelt before quickly shoveling the pile into the bucket, scraping the cobblestone street clean until only a wet spot remained. He then placed the shovel in the bucket and headed toward the front door.

Lord Saxon's hand on his shoulder stopped him. "You are not carrying that through the house. Walk around the block to the back door." He released Charles, clicked his tongue in disgust and headed back inside the house. He turned, shaking his head as he closed the massive front door behind him.

Charles gave a heavy sigh and started down the block. He was good enough to use the front door to save the master's family face, it seemed, but not good enough to use it to do his job. The cold October wind blew, chilling him as he carried the manure down the block to the alleyway.

He'd started working for the Saxon family when he was ten. Twelve years later, he was doing heavier work that was needed around the house.

Burton Roberts was the butler. He answered the front door and announced visitors. Burton saw to the running of the home and to ordering Charles around.

As to Lord Sebastian Saxon, he was a banker and came from old money. His mother still lived in the west wing of the home, but no one ever saw her. She had her own personal servant. Lord Saxon's wife, Lady Margaret Saxon, was away visiting the country estate with their two younger daughters. Thomas Saxon, their eldest son, was twenty-three, a year older than Charles, and was in training to learn the family banking business.

When Charles turned thirteen, he was old enough to permanently leave home and move into the Saxon's main house with a room on the third floor.

Thomas Saxon had been thrilled to have someone his own age in the house. When there wasn't work to be done, Thomas would seek out Charles for company, even sneaking out of his room at night to head up to the third floor to sleep in Charles's room.

Lord Saxon discovered his son's activities and tried to put a stop to them, but Thomas knew all the secret passageways in the house. Though one night, years into his nightly visits, the younger Saxon discovered something about himself and Charles that his father couldn't possibly have known: they both enjoyed the attention of the same sex.

As his father droned on and on about the position he would have in society and about the woman he would some day marry, Thomas would look at Charles with desire burning in his eyes, while Charles, on the other hand, would look away in utter disdain.

After all, he knew his station in life and hated the attention Thomas placed on him. Thomas, for his part, thought it was a game Charles played with him, but Charles simply did not like him, did not like that, with age, Thomas like his father had turned cold and mean, frequently forcing the servant to do whatever he wanted, whenever he wanted. Charles only obeyed in fear of Lord Saxon finding out. Suffice it to say, he desperately needed his job to help support his family.

The smell of the fresh manure was strong until Charles turned down the alley. The breeze blew into his face, chilling him even more, but it also pushed the stench away from him. He took a deep breath of fresh air and hurried to the back door, then emptied and rinsed the bucket before returning it to the pantry.

"Lord Saxon said you were too slow cleaning up the mess," Mrs. March scolded.

"I'm sorry," Charles replied as he bowed his head.

Mrs. Marsh grumbled in response. "In any case, Lord Saxon wants to see you in his study, now. Wash your hands and carry this tray of tea up to him. Maybe that will calm his temper." She pointed to the silver tray on the counter.

Charles did as was told, slipping on a pair of white gloves before picking up the tray. He balanced the contents up the narrow steps and headed to the study.

Thomas was waiting for him in the hallway. He pulled his pants tight in front so that the material hugged his bulge and showed his aroused state as he picked a biscuit off the tray. He took a bite and let the crumbs fall onto the floor. "Father has a meeting this afternoon, and, so far, I do not have to attend..." His words hung in the air as he turned his rump to Charles before giving it a solid thwack.

Charles knocked on the study door and turned the knob before Thomas could say anything else. After all, he already knew what the young master wanted.

"Come in," Lord Saxon called as the door opened. He glanced up from the papers he was reading. "Charles..." He stopped when he saw the tray. "I didn't...oh, never mind, bring it over. Mrs. Marsh must have thought I needed all this." He sighed. "Come closer, I need to tell you something."

Charles neared the mahogany desk and set the tray upon it. He trained his eyes down to the floor.

"Charles, I have hired a driver. He is to start today. He needs a room to stay in, and yours is the only one with an open spare bed, apart from the one in the garage, and that room has no furniture."

Charles almost gasped, but held his reaction in.

"He will be sharing with you; make him feel welcome."

Charles knew he had no choice, but was glad it was simply a new roommate instead of a scolding for being slow or using the front door.

"He should arrive before noon. Help him carry his things in, show him where everything is and introduce him to the other staff." Lord Saxon looked back down at his papers, thereby dismissing him.

Charles nodded and backed away.

"If you see Thomas, send him in; he needs to attend this meeting with me." Lord Saxon didn't look up from his work as he continued his reading.

Charles left the room and headed back downstairs to the kitchen.

Thomas jumped out of an alcove and pressed his body against Charles's back. He thrust his throbbing member between Charles's tight cheeks. "You know you want it," he rasped.

"Your father wants to see you." Charles remained motionless as he allowed Thomas to rub against him.

"Tell him you couldn't find me." His hand moved closer to Charles's groin.

"Thomas!" Lord Saxon's voice boomed from the study.

Thomas immediately released Charles and pushed him away. He then wiped his hands as if he had been soiled and sneered as he headed to the study. "I'll find you later," he said over his shoulder.

Charles forced himself to slowly walk away, never letting Thomas know how much he wanted to bolt from him. He smiled to himself. Thomas would find out he had a new roommate, and that, he prayed, would make his own life a little simpler.

Wesley Holmes arrived at the back door promptly at eleven. He wore his black suit and his hat was pulled down low on his head. Mrs. Marsh rushed around getting the lunch ready for the staff, while Lord Saxon and Thomas finally left for their meeting. Thomas complained the entire time, looked longingly at Charles all the while.

Charles breathed a sigh of relief when they left. He was polishing the silver when Wesley arrived.

"I don't have time to help you right now, Charles." Mrs. Marsh stirred the soup so it wouldn't scorch. "Why I chose a cream of potato soup for today is beyond me," she complained to the swirling broth below.

Charles set his cloth and spoon down and greeted Wesley. "Hello, I'm Charles. Lord Saxon asked me to help you settle in."

As Wesley pulled his hat off, his blond hair tumbled out. His blue eyes glowed with the warmth of a summer sky, and his body, it appeared, was tight and muscular.

"Lunch will be served in ten minutes, so no dawdling." Mrs. Marsh shook her spoon at the both of them.

Charles bent over and picked up one of Wesley's suitcases. "You'll be sharing a room with me; I'll show you where it is." Charles headed to the narrow staircase that led up to the third floor.

Wesley picked up his other case and box and followed him.

As they climbed to the third floor, the temperature also rose.

"In the winter the upstairs is warm all day but cools off at night, while in the summer it's always hot." He opened the door and walked down the hallway to his room—their room. He pushed the door open and set the suitcase on the unmade bed. "Sara was supposed to have fresh linens on your bed."

"I can make my own bed. Just show me where the sheets are kept." Wesley set his other case on the bed and the box on the floor. "Which chest of drawers is yours?"

Charles pointed to the one by the door. "I can switch to the other one if you'd like."

"The open one is fine. What about the wardrobe?" Wesley opened the doors.

Charles's clothes hung on both sides. He pushed them to one side and said, "That half is all yours."

"Thank you." Wesley looked around the room. "You've been alone in here a long time. I'm sorry to suddenly invade."

Charles smiled. "I'm glad to have a roommate. The nights can get long sometimes."

Wesley picked up the nearby pitcher and poured water into the basin. Quickly, he washed his face and hands. "Okay then, I suppose I'm ready for lunch."

"Dear me," cried Charles. "We'd better hurry before Mrs. Marsh skins us alive for being late."

They raced down the stairs and burst into the kitchen just as Mrs. Marsh set the last bowl on the table.

Burton stood at the front chair and pointed to his right. "This will be your seat, Wesley, next to Charles."

Wesley took his place and waited for the female staff to sit before he did.

Burton nodded as the women sat and the meal began.

Charles didn't have to introduce the staff to Wesley. One by one, they offered their names and positions in the house. The women eyed Wesley's good looks with a sidewise glance, batting their eyelashes as they coyly welcomed him to the house.

Sara, the upstairs maid, Ingrid, the cook's assistant, Paul, the valet, Mary, the ladies' maid, Molly, the scullery maid, Donald, the footman, all made up the ranks of the house, along, of course, with Burton, Charles and now Wesley.

Wesley ate quickly, memorizing the names and positions. He looked at Charles and noticed his intent look as he finished his meal. Wesley's leg brushed against Charles's under the table, and he felt a stirring in his pants. He reached down to scratch the spot, touching Charles's leg as he did so. He then quickly pulled away as if burned.

Burton frowned at the sudden motion, but wasn't sure what had happened, while Charles simply picked up his dishes and carried them to the sink.

Wesley followed his example and set his dishes on top of Charles's. "Are you allowed to give me a tour of the house or is that part of Burton or Lord Saxon's responsibility?"

Burton entered at that very moment. "Charles, if you are done with your chores, take him around the house. I have a few tasks to complete before Lord Saxon returns from his meeting." He set his dish on the ever-growing pile.

Charles smiled. "We'll start on the main floor and head up to the third, and then we'll come back down here to see the servant area."

Wesley nodded and followed Charles. They walked to the library first. Charles opened the door. Wesley gasped as he saw the floor-to-ceiling bookshelves. Rows and rows of leather-bound books lined the richly appointed room.

"Lord Saxon will allow us to take a book to read if we want, but we must take extra care with them." Charles ran his finger along the spine of a volume of poems.

Wesley inhaled deeply. "I love the smell of books."

Charles smiled. "As do I." He stepped out of the library and headed to Lord Saxon's study. He opened the door, but did not enter. "Only Sara is allowed in here to clean, and only when Lord Saxon has ordered it."

Wesley nodded and stepped back, while Charles closed the study door and walked to the entryway and front door. "We are not allowed to use the front door." Charles touched the doorknob and stopped. He did not dare open it. Instead, he headed to the formal dining room. Candles sat in the center of the table, and plates and silverware lined the sides. "Meals are served at seven; staff eats afterward."

Wesley looked around the wood panels and portraits that lined the walls. Fine crystal glasses and vases waited for water and flowers as the table was set for the evening.

"Through here are the formal living room and the parlor. The appropriate room is chosen depending on the guests." Charles waited for Wesley to take all the grandeur in.

Wesley followed Charles to the doors and peeked into the living room and parlor. "I'm not sure what Lord Saxon wants me to do when I'm not driving or running errands, but if anyone needs help with anything, please let me know. After all, this place is enormous."

They headed back to the main entrance before ascending the grand staircase. Finely carved wood formed the railing, which curved and circled up to the second floor.

"The family and guest bedrooms are on the second floor. Lord Saxon has one rule: no men in the women's rooms and no women in the men's. He is afraid of scandal. One diplomat decided to entertain in his room, and Lord Saxon paid a healthy price to keep that story under wraps."

"I'm sure his personal image reflects on the bank."

Charles nodded. "With rumors of war whispered all through the society pages, he could lose everything if there was a run on the bank or if there was even a hint of impropriety."

They walked along the overlook to the grand entrance and entered the hall of bedrooms. "The master bedroom faces the street. Lord Saxon has his own private room, and next to it is Lady Saxon's. Her suite has massive closets to hold all of her clothing, and there's even a room the seamstress uses to sew her gowns. The girls' nursery is across the hall from her Lady's room, and Master Thomas's room is across from his father's. He has a balcony off his room that overlooks the stables."

Wesley walked to Thomas's room and opened the door. A strong male scent filled the air, along with smoke and cedar. He turned to face Charles. "You have something to say about him, don't you?" His eyes burned a cold blue, demanding to be told the truth.

"Master Thomas has his, well, *ways*." Charles could feel his face begin to burn.

Wesley walked closer to Charles and touched his shoulder. "I'm sorry. I will figure these things out for myself, I suppose. I don't mean to—"

"I would be careful of Thomas," Charles blurted out. "He has had many good people fired, and without any references. They will never find a job in this country after he has ruined them."

Wesley looked shocked and quickly left the room, walking down the hallway instead. "And the rooms at the end of the hall?"

"Those are for the guests who stay overnight. Fresh linens are put on the beds weekly, even if they haven't been used."

"The poor maids," Wesley said.

"It gives us a job."

Wesley nodded. "I gather that Lord Saxon is very picky, so I will never have a dirty car for him to drive in and I'll wear only the whitest gloves, and no spots on my uniform."

Charles also nodded, but quickly frowned when he heard Thomas coming up the stairs.

"Father, I need to get something from my room," the young master yelled down the stairway as he ran up to the second floor.

Charles grabbed Wesley's hand and pulled him through a panel in the hallway. The passage led to a staircase rising to the third floor. The door at the top opened directly next to their bedroom.

Wesley looked stunned, and then realization set in: Thomas was clearly one to avoid.

Charles let go of the other man's hand, but Wesley held on for a second longer. He looked into Charles's eyes. "I need to change into a clean uniform before I meet Lord Saxon." He waited for Charles to open their bedroom door before following him inside. He took off his coat and turned it over in his hands. No spots or stains. He looked down at his black pants and noticed a smudge on the knee. He unbuckled his belt. "Could you help me?"

Charles swallowed hard. "Excuse me?"

"I haven't unpacked, and I need a fresh pair of pants. Can you open my cases and find one?" Wesley unbuttoned his trousers and bent to untie his shoes.

Charles noticed his firm rump as the pants rode deep into his crease. He promptly turned as he felt his arousal grow. Opening the first case, he found sheer white underwear. His fingers fondled the soft fabric as he pulled them out to look underneath. His arousal grew to full length, his face flaming as he dug through his new roommate's personal things, but he quickly found a neatly folded pair of black pants and carefully removed them.

Wesley, in the meantime, had removed his soiled pants and was pulling off his shirt, just as Charles turned his way. His hairy chest was covered in a thick pelt that disappeared into his sheer underwear. A black triangle of hair could easily be seen through the fabric, as could the penis and balls pressed tightly within.

It was impossible for Charles not to notice how handsome the man standing before him was.

"Can you find a new white shirt, too?" Wesley stepped closer, causing his fly to pull open and part of his thick, fleshy shaft to slip through the opening, pink against a sea of white.

Charles couldn't resist any longer. His hand reached out and touched the thick mass of hair on Wesley's chest. His fingers combed through the tangles and cupped his pec. Finding Wesley's nipple hard, he gently pinched it. His other hand traced down the torso to the exposed flesh below. His hand felt the heat of Wesley's sex. The cock within slipped out of the shorts and filled his palm. A pearl of wetness bubbled up.

Wesley moved even closer, his mouth opening as his lips sought Charles's. As they touched, heat blazed between them.

Charles stroked Wesley's hard prick, caressing every inch. He explored the wet opening, where more spunk was seeping out. His kiss intensified as he felt Wesley's body melt against his own.

"Charles?" Thomas's voice suddenly called from the hallway.

Instantly, Charles released the cock from his grip and rushed to the suitcase to find a shirt, wiping his mouth with the back of his hand, especially since the hot, slick sap covered his palm. He tasted the salty-sweetness and savored its flavor.

Wesley slipped his hard dick back inside his shorts as the bedroom door burst open. He turned his back to Thomas.

"You didn't knock. You shouldn't barge into a room like that." Wesley stepped into his pants, and once his throbbing member was covered, he turned and faced his new employer.

Thomas's eyes scanned Wesley's beautiful torso up and down. "Sorry, I didn't realize you were changing." His gaze lingered on the bulging groin as he bit his lower lip. He extended his hand. "You must be Wesley, our new driver." His face flushed with desire.

Charles felt sick watching the scene unfold. He pulled out a white shirt and quickly unbuttoned it, then walked over to Wesley, standing between him and Thomas as he handed the shirt over.

"Thank you for your help, Charles. I'll have to unpack after supper." He slipped the shirt over one arm and around his back.

Thomas's brow furrowed once the shirt covered Wesley's hairy chest. "Make one of the maids do that for you," he said.

"Female staff aren't allowed—" Charles started to say.

"I think you'll need your own room, too." Thomas continued to stare as Wesley buttoned his shirt. He fairly swooned when Wesley tucked his shirttails into his pants.

"There aren't any available," Charles informed him.

"Our driver must be closer to the family, in case of an emergency."

Charles felt an empty sinking feeling in his stomach.

"This room is fine," Wesley interrupted, "and Charles is my friend. I enjoy his company."

Thomas glared at Charles. "We'll see about that." He turned on his heel and stormed out the door.

"That didn't go too well," Charles said with a frown.

"His father hired me," Wesley reminded him. "Thomas has nothing to do with it." And again the distance between them was closed, the kiss at last repeated.

\* \* \*

Ten minutes later, Charles knocked on Lord Saxon's study door.

"Come in," his employer shouted.

Charles opened the door and waited for Wesley to enter. His roommate was now dressed and pressed and looked perfect.

"Your driver has arrived." Charles bowed as he backed away.

"Wesley, I hear you're settled in upstairs." Lord Saxon finally looked up from the ledger he was writing in.

"Yes, sir. Charles has been most kind to—"

"I want you to live in the room off of the garage." Lord Saxon looked down at his book and again started writing.

"If I may, sir," Wesley said, "I inhale the fumes all day driving; I prefer not to breathe them in while I sleep."

Lord Saxon stopped writing. He held his pen firmly in hand and slowly looked up at his driver. His eyes narrowed as his forehead creased. "Do you dare question my orders?"

"No, sir," coughed out Wesley. "I will be available at a moment's notice, sir, and being upstairs in the house versus the garage will only speed things up when you need me. Living in the garage would actually slow them down, I believe. That's all I meant to say."

Lord Saxon inhaled and exhaled. His eyes rolled up as he said, "Fine. Stay where you are then. We'll see how this arrangement works out. Oh, and welcome to our home." He waved his hand, dismissing the men in his presence.

Charles headed out of the room, and Wesley followed. "Let me show you the garage, and then you can get started organizing it the way you want." He led them down the stairs and through the kitchen. The garage was detached from the house. As he raised the large door, he saw Thomas standing by the car.

"That will be all, Charles," he said.

"But I need to show him where the keys and tools are."

"I'll take care of that." Thomas moved closer to the chauffeur.

"Master Thomas, your father wants you in his study," Mrs. Marsh called from the house's back door.

Thomas's face darkened as he ground his teeth. "When I return, I'll need a ride."

Wesley nodded. "I'll be ready whenever you get here, sir." He smiled and watched Thomas leave to go back into the house.

"I need you at the front door. I'm not being picked up back here," Thomas yelled over his shoulder as he hurried inside the house.

Charles opened a cabinet above a workbench, glad that Thomas had finally left them alone together. "The keys are up here for everything you'll need. All the tools are in the workbench, and that door leads to the spare room."

Wesley walked into the spare room and looked around. There was more light, more space, but still he was glad that he was rooming with Charles.

The afternoon raced by, and soon supper was over. The staff was settling down for the night.

"We can bathe before bed or in the morning, whichever you prefer. Most of the staff just wash up in their rooms, but there is a bathtub in the laundry room. You can bathe there anytime, but just make sure you lock the door." Charles showed him the bathtub.

"I think I'll take a pitcher of hot water up to our room. I want to unpack and clean up before bed," Wesley said.

Charles grabbed a bucket and filled it with the hot water. "I'll carry it up for you."

"Thank you," Wesley said. He bid good night to the other staff in the kitchen and then followed Charles up the stairs. He opened the door and waited for Charles to pass by with the bucket. Once inside, he locked the door and stripped off his pants and shirt. He stood in his sheer underwear, quickly folding his clothes.

"Do you need any help?" Charles asked. He scanned every inch of Wesley's body, enjoying the hair, the muscles, the man.

"If you want to put my underwear and socks in the drawers, I can hang up my clothes in the wardrobe." Wesley hurried to hang up his clothes.

"Do you need a robe?" Charles asked as his erection slowly grew.

"Is my being in my underwear an issue?" Wesley asked, with a crooked grin. He bent over to pick up a hanger from the floor, his ass stretching the fabric across his cheeks.

Charles could see the hair that lined his crease, his pink pucker easily seen as well. "No, I'm fine," he croaked out.

Wesley laughed as he placed his last shirt into the wardrobe. "I just want to wash up and get into bed."

Charles put the last pair of shorts into the top drawer and closed it. "Done."

Wesley slid the empty suitcases under his bed and walked over to the bucket of hot water. He tossed in a washcloth and started to scrub under his arms. The thick hair began to mat on his body and stick to his skin.

Charles watched as the water beaded and rolled down his beautiful torso before soaking into his shorts. As the sheer material turned wet, it became even easier to see through it. Wesley's ass flexed with each motion he made.

Charles had to take off his jacket and shirt because it was suddenly too hot in the room. His shoes and pants disappeared next.

"I hope these dry by morning." Wesley slipped his shorts off and hung them over the back of the chair. His naked body was perfect, Charles couldn't help but notice. He then washed between his legs and his hairy sack, his cock standing straight out as he wiped between his asscheeks. Lastly, he washed his long hairy legs and turned to look for a towel.

Charles closed his eyes. He couldn't take it anymore. When he opened them, Wesley was in his bed, covers pulled up to his chin. Charles quickly finished putting his own clothes away and blew out the candle.

By then, the fire had burned down to embers in their room. Charles placed a log on the grate before he slipped into his bed and tried to sleep. He could hear the rhythmic breathing of Wesley, and he exhaled the air he'd been holding.

"Thank you for all your help today," Wesley said. "If there's anything I can do for you, just let me know."

Charles's cock ached as he rolled over onto his side, with his back to Wesley. He knew he wouldn't sleep tonight. A cool draft suddenly blew down his back. He turned to see what was causing it.

Wesley's naked body slipped under the sheets and his hairy arms wrapped around Charles, holding him tightly. Wesley's hard dick rested between Charles's smooth cheeks as Wesley's hand caressed down the other man's body. Lower and lower his hand explored.

Charles held his breath as Wesley's deft fingers combed through his pubic bush. His cock trembled, oozing spunk.

Wesley felt a thick drop land on his hand as he wrapped his fingers around Charles's shaft, and a gentle stroke began.

Charles moaned with pleasure. No one had ever been so tender and caring, so loving. Only a rushed, forced touch was known to him in the past.

"Relax," Wesley breathed into his ear. "I want to make this last." His tongue licked the proffered lobe and he bit it gently.

His hand milked out more sticky sap. He brought it to his mouth and tasted it. "I want you."

Charles pushed back against him. "I want that, too. I want to be inside of you." Charles almost spent then and there as he rolled onto his back.

Wesley moved on top of him and kissed him deeper. Their tongues dueled as their cocks slid alongside each other. Wesley ground his pelvis into Charles. He spread his legs and moved higher up as Charles's dick slipped between his cheeks. He rode him like that as they kissed.

Wesley's hair was still damp from the sponge bath and his crease was still slippery from the soap. He moved up and down again, lining his pucker up over Charles's fat mushroom head. He rocked back and forth, trying to relax and to allow Charles's girth to enter him. He was tight, and Charles was quite large.

The prone man moaned as he felt his tip enter the hot, hairy opening. More sap poured out and lubed the tight spot. Charles thrust his hips to help Wesley along, while Wesley took a deep breath and plunged back in return.

Charles pressed forward and the fat head probed deeper inside.

Wesley's pain turned into a warm feeling, which grew deep inside him as, inch by inch, the thick prick filled him.

Charles arched his back as his hairy balls pressed against Wesley's ass, his whole length inside now. He held his breath, afraid to move, to cause the explosion that was rapidly building.

Wesley started to slowly move. He pulled Charles's tongue inside his mouth and sucked as hard as he could.

Charles followed, savoring the moment. Slowly, he felt Wesley rise up, breaking their kiss.

Wesley leaned back and forced Charles deeper inside himself. He started to ride the man below him.

Charles reached down and grabbed Wesley's bouncing dick, and a stroke was administered, growing faster as their pace increased. He felt the sticky flow across his palm, making Wesley's cock glide even easier.

Sweat started to roll over their bodies. The scent of manly sex rose from them both. Their breathing came in quick violent gasps. Charles bit down on his lip, trying to make this last. He squeezed harder on Wesley's cock, and it suddenly sprayed his chest.

The hot load filled his hand as it continued to shoot across his body. A drop landed on his lips, and he licked it away, swallowing the sweet ambrosia.

Charles then felt his dick explode inside, filling Wesley to his core. Wave after wave of pleasure slammed into Wesley's prostate gland, driving another orgasm out and over Charles.

The man on top leaned down and kissed the one below. The sensation was too much, and he collapsed on top of him. Their chests heaved as they struggled to regain their breaths. Sweat and semen ran over their bodies as they held each other.

Charles snuggled against Wesley. Slowly, they drifted off to sleep in each other's arms.

Midmorning the next day, Thomas snapped his fingers at his chauffeur. "Wesley, I need a ride to the bank."

"Right away, sir." Wesley put his cap on and headed out the back door. He drove around the block and parked in front of the house. Once there, he waited and waited.

Thomas never came out.

He gazed down at the horn, but thought the better of it. He walked up to the front door and rang the bell instead.

Burton opened the door, looking confused. "Wesley, you know you must use the back door."

"I've been waiting for Master Thomas out front. He wanted a ride to the bank," Wesley explained as he entered the hallway.

Thomas came out of the library. "Burton, is there a problem?"

"No, sir," Burton replied. "Wesley said that you needed a ride, and has been waiting for you."

"Wesley, why are you using the front door? You know what my father thinks of that," Thomas scolded.

"I'm sorry, sir. I just wanted you to know I was here. I'd hate for you to have to wait for me." Wesley's face flushed as he spoke.

"Well, I'm ready for that ride now." Thomas walked to the front door.

Wesley also started toward the front door just as Charles came down the stairs.

"Didn't we just talk about you not using the front door?" Thomas asked, anger burning in his eyes now.

"But I..." and Wesley stopped. "Right away, sir." He tipped his hat and headed over to Charles on the stairs.

Charles stopped him. "Thomas, do you really want him to run all the way around the block to get to the car?"

"That is his job." Thomas smiled, coldly. He approached Charles and trapped him against the banister.

"What I—" Charles started, but Thomas put one hand to his chest and grabbed his balls with the other. He pushed harder against Charles's body and pinned him there in pain.

"Don't hurt him. It's okay," Wesley said, nervously. "I'll be outside in just a moment, sir."

"Well, make it snappy." Thomas removed his hand from Charles's chest and clicked his fingers, still squeezing the balls all the while.

Charles groaned in obvious pain.

Wesley headed for the stairs.

"Thomas, it's not the door that the man enters or leaves through that makes him what he is; it's the integrity of the man inside that makes him that," Charles said through clenched teeth.

Wesley stopped on the stairway and walked back up to Thomas. "Please, don't take this out on him. He's done nothing wrong."

"He's my servant, as are you, and I'll do as I see fit." Thomas released Charles and turned to grab Wesley.

Charles reached down to rub the blood back into his groin and then turned and spotted Lord Saxon standing in the hallway next to Burton.

"Thomas! Don't you even think about that," Lord Saxon commanded.

"Sorry, sir," Wesley said, afraid that the lord's wrath would fall on him next.

"Charles, Wesley, Burton, you may go back about your business. I need to speak to my son, *alone*. He needs to understand integrity." Lord Saxon waited for his son and led him to his study. As he closed the door, the others heard him say, "We need to talk about you moving out to the country estate..."

Burton hurried off the dining room to check on the settings.

Wesley and Charles walked down the stairs and gladly closed the door behind them.

# CHAUFFEUR'S
# HOLE

**Landon Dixon**

Lord Duffield handed his top hat and gloves to Colburn, and then unbuttoned his greatcoat. "So, how have things been here, Colburn, while I've been away?"

The elderly butler helped his master off with the greatcoat before replying, "Everything has been fine here, my Lord. I'm sure Lady Duffield will be telling you the same." There was just a hint of irony in the stone-faced man's voice, which his Lordship didn't fail to pick up on.

Duffield glanced at Colburn, ran his fingers through his thick, black hair and briefly fondled the ends of his dark moustache. "Yes, I'm sure that she will. Where, pray tell, is her Ladyship, by the way?"

"She's attending the Edinburgh Charity Society annual function tonight, my Lord. Otherwise, she would have met you at the train herself. She said she'd be returning around midnight."

"Fine. That will be all then, Colburn."

The butler frowned. "Um, there's a man waiting to see you in the sitting room, my Lord. He said his name was Albert Pinker, and that you were expecting him. I tried to tell him that—"

"That's all right, Colburn; I'll see him at once."

Lord Duffield strode purposefully away down the dark-paneled hallway, flung open the oaken door of the sitting room and walked inside.

Albert Pinker pushed himself up out of a deep, green leather chair with a wheeze and turned to face Duffield. "Ah, Lord Duffield. How are the plantations in India, sir?"

"Prodigiously producing tea, I'm happy to report, Mr. Pinker." He waved the man back down into his chair and then threw his own trim form onto the red leather couch across from him. "Now, what of *your* report, Mr. Pinker?"

The detective was a short, stocky man with a bald head and a bushy moustache as well as a florid face and clear blue eyes. He was dressed in a tight-fitting blue serge suit and black bow tie. He pulled a thick brown leather notebook out of the breast pocket of his suit jacket, flipped it open and began reading. "The evening of your departure, August Sixteenth, her Lady-ship left the house at eight at night to attend a performance of 'The Mi-kado' at the new Usher Hall. She met three women in the lobby of the hall, the—"

"McIntyre sisters. Yes, yes, Pinker, there's no need to go through all the humdrum details. I'm sure you're very thor-ough in your work. But just get to the—well, anything out of the ordinary that might have occurred." Duffield twisted his large hands in his lap, his bright brown eyes hooded, before he suddenly jumped up and walked over to the small bar next to the huge fireplace. "Perhaps you'd like a wee dram of—"

"Never touch the stuff, sir," Pinker brusquely replied, flip-ping pages in his notebook.

"Well, I could certainly use a drink," Duffield murmured to

himself. He splashed a generous quantity of scotch into a crystal tumbler and then sat back down, waiting impatiently for Pinker to get to the point.

"Ah, here we go, sir." The detective cleared his throat as Duffield nervously filled his glass. "Two in the afternoon, August Seventeenth, your wife left the house in the car with the chauffeur, Robert Kinnaird. I hailed a taxi and followed. After touring the streets around Old Town, they drove out past the city limits to Eden Wood and then stopped at the far end of the park under some large trees. I followed on foot and took up a vantage point behind some bushes approximately one hundred feet away from the parked vehicle, whereupon I observed Kinnaird get out of the front seat and get into the back—*with* her Ladyship."

Pinker glanced up, his ruddy face coloring still more.

Duffield stared straight ahead, clutching his empty whiskey glass.

"I then observed the pair embracing, kissing, and...*frenching*, I believe it's called on the continent, sir. Kinnaird helped her Ladyship pull down the top of her dress and then he gripped her bare—"

"Did he have intercourse with my wife, Mr. Pinker?"

The detective looked up, somewhat reluctantly, from his detailed notes. "Yes, sir," he stated. "He did."

Duffield looked down. "In...the usual manner, I suppose?"

"In the backseat of the car, sir, as I just—"

"No! I mean...in the usual *position*?"

"Not quite, sir," Pinker replied. "He used the chauffeur's hole."

Duffield stared at the detective, puzzled. "The 'chauffeur's hole'?"

"That's what we call it in the business, sir. The, uh...*anus*, in medical terms. It's not uncommon, you see, sir, for a wife, when she has an affair, to take it up the bum, so to speak. That way, there can be no question of, uh, complications—pregnancy, you know. And since many, well, younger wives nowadays have affairs with their chauffeurs—since the advent of the automobile—we in the business have taken to calling it—"

"Yes, all right, Pinker." Duffield was all too aware of the twenty-odd-year age gap between himself and his wife, Katherine. "Mr. Kinnaird, is he...well-endowed?"

"Why, yes, sir, I'd say so, from what I observed," Pinker responded hesitantly, thrown off guard by the question. "There *was* a rather loud groan, when he, uh, *penetrated* your wife, sir."

"And did he seem to enjoy...the act?"

"He? Uh, well, *he* seemed to come away...*satisfied*, I should describe it, sir."

Duffield rose and walked over to the bar and set his glass down. "Did it happen again?"

"Ten more times, sir," Pinker dutifully reported. "During the fortnight you were away. In the car, on the bank of a stream, behind—"

"But always in the...chauffeur's hole?"

"Yes, sir. You may notice her Ladyship's gait is somewhat—"

Duffield swung around. "That will be all, thank you, Mr. Pinker. Please get your firm to send me an account for your services."

As the two men shook hands, the detective took note of the dampness of Lord Duffield's palm, the slight tremor in his hand and the definite bulge in his Lordship's tweed trousers.

When Pinker at last departed, Duffield fortified himself with another large tumbler of scotch. Then he exited the sitting room, walked back up the hallway, turned left and went down the steep staircase that led to the servants' quarters.

Duffield walked down the narrow, darkened corridor to the last door on the right. He looked back at the deserted hallway, then reached up and shifted aside the small, round, steel covering on the eye-level opening affixed within the door before peering into the chauffeur's room through the tiny porthole.

The small room was sparsely furnished with an iron-railed bed, a tall, narrow wardrobe, a squat chest of drawers with an enamel washbasin and a jug on top, and a wooden desk and chair. Robert Kinnaird was standing in the middle of the room, preparing for bed. He was already bare-chested, pushing down his trousers, and appeared not to have heard the slight scraping of the peephole as it was uncovered. The chauffeur skinned down his cotton undergarments, stepped out of his trousers and underthings and was suddenly completely naked.

Duffield's eye widened, pressed as it was against the glass aperture. His cock swelled to full, throbbing length inside his trousers as he stared at Kinnaird's bared cock, which dangled a good four inches down from the man's loins—soft—hanging over large, ginger-fuzzed balls.

The rest of the man's nude body was built lean and long and well proportioned, his skin the color and smoothness of alabaster, his nipples puffy and coral pink. He was standing sideways to his spying master, his young buttocks thrusting out round and taut behind him. The short red hair on his head was parted to one side and his chiseled face was clean shaven.

Duffield swallowed hard, dizzy at the stark-naked sight of his servant, a rush of blood engorging his own still-covered cock. He stole another quick glance down the empty corridor. All of the doors along the hallway were closed, no lights showing beneath. He reaffixed his eye to the glass opening, then backed his body up slightly, reached down, unbuttoned his trousers and pulled his enormous erection out of his undergarments. He gripped the swollen member with his right hand and cupped his hairy balls with his left. Then he stroked his pulsating cock and squeezed his tingling balls, his eye once again glued to Kinnaird in the bedroom.

The chauffeur picked his coat, collar, bow tie and shirt up off the bed and hung them up in the wardrobe, then retrieved his pants and undergarments from off the floor and draped them over the chair. As he did so, he turned his back on the peeping master of the house and slightly bent over. Duffield gaped at the full moon view of Kinnaird's buttocks.

Kinnaird removed something from a trouser pocket and turned sideways to Duffield again. He fanned a sheaf of banknotes out in his hands, smiling all the while. Then the man cupped all of the banknotes in his right hand, grasped his cock with the same hand, along with the notes, and began stroking. His grin widened as his cock rapidly thickened and lengthened with the banknotes' caress. He fingered one of his nipples with his other hand, pinching the prominent protuberance.

Duffield stared on, incensed, fisting his own cock, twisting his balls, his breath locked in his burning lungs and his body and face blazing. His chauffeur appeared to have an insatiable appetite for both shared and solo pleasure, and Duffield could well surmise where the handsome, hung young man had gotten that sheaf of lucky stroking notes.

Kinnaird dropped his hand off his chest and pulled a single banknote out of the bunch that was still curved around his turgid shaft. He placed the note on the bed, then aimed the curved crown of his cock at it, pumping his full-blown erection with long, hard, urgent tugs while juggling his balls with his other set of fingers.

Duffield's overlarge hand flew on his overlarge cock, his balls squeezed in a vise, his entire body surging to climax.

Kinnaird jerked, grunted and threw back his head. Semen spurted out the tip of his jacked cock and striped down onto the single banknote. At the same time, Duffield spasmed and groaned, spraying a hot, heady blast of ejaculate out of his handled cock that splashed against the servant's door, his balls pulsing in his other clutching hand.

The two men were jolted repeatedly with the joys of self-pleasure, the one taking out his satisfaction with his money, the other coating the door with his heated delight as he spied on his servant. Kinnaird's huge organ jumped and spouted in his hand, his body convulsing with each ecstatic jet, while Duffield doused his frustration in a hose-load of semen, his eye riveted to Kinnaird and his still-shooting cock.

Before Robert Kinnaird could clean up his mess, Lord Duffield burst the door open and bulled into the room—as was his right as master of the house, his duty as aggrieved husband of a young wife.

"You've been dallying with her Ladyship, sir!" he thundered at Kinnaird. "She gave you that money in return for your silence—and services, I dare say!"

Kinnaird took a step backward away from his blustering master. But despite his vulnerable nakedness, despite the swollen appendage jutting flagrantly out from between his legs, and the semen-slathered banknote on the bed and the more in his hand—not to mention the truth of his Lordship's accusing words—the man smiled easily and nodded, his composure hardly ruffled at all. For he'd shrewdly noticed the still sizable bulge in Duffield's trousers, the round stain on the tweed, and the older man's glaring eyes, which were fixated on his own cock. Also, he possessed the knowledge Lady Katherine had imparted to him in moments of intimacy, which was flimsy justification for her moral turpitude: that Duffield had married her only that he might have a charming hostess for entertaining Edinburgh's elite and that his affections did not extend to the bedroom.

"What you say is true, sir," Kinnaird admitted, his green eyes twinkling. "But the favor goes *both ways*, if you get my meaning." He turned his back on Duffield and bent forward at the waist, thrusting his buttocks out at his Lordship in a bold, blatant, provocative manner.

Duffield stared at the perfect pair on display, served up right before him. He swallowed, stepped forward, stretched out his hand and touched a trembling finger to a fine, young, fleshy cheek. Kinnaird shivered, causing his buttocks to dance.

Duffield jerked his hand back and chewed his lip, suffused with shimmering warmth at the smooth, hot feel of the other man's ass and at the proffered invitation. His cock strained the buttons of his trousers again, his eyes blinded by the dazzling white humps before him. He blundered down to his knees and grabbed on to the man's buttocks, thrusting his reddened face in between the smothering hillocks.

Kinnaird quivered and smiled, feeling his master's strong hands knead his cheeks, his master's hot breath flooding his crack. Duffield pulled the meaty pair apart and stuck his tongue in deep, licking the smooth, pink, sensitive skin of the other man's crack. Kinnaird jumped and moaned, his buttocks rippling, while Duffield excitedly grasped and lapped.

His Lordship licked and licked his chauffeur's rump, his eager tongue slapping the crack up and down before twirling the tip around the puckered opening to Kinnaird's anus. He then speared his tongue directly into Kinnaird's chute and spiraled it around inside the man. The chauffeur groaned and bucked in response.

After urgently rimming Kinnaird's tender hole, Duffield

finally pulled back, gasping for air. He turned Kinnaird around by his trim hips, the man's cock towering out, purple capped and pink shafted, the slit glistening. Duffield wrapped the fingers of his right hand around the thick shaft and began to steadily pump away at it.

Kinnaird moaned and arched, thrusting his organ out even farther into Duffield's hand and face. Duffield stared into the yawning slit within the bloated hood, feeling the heat and the beat of the shaft beneath his shifting hand. He cupped Kinnaird's hanging balls with his left hand, hefted them, squeezed them, rolled them between his twitching fingers while pumping Kinnaird's pipe with his other hand.

At last, the master pushed his head forward and parted his red lips wider and took Kinnaird's mushroomed hood directly into his mouth.

"Yes, my Lord!" the chauffeur shouted, jerking, sliding more of his cock into his master's mouth.

Duffield consumed as much of the mammoth member as he could, then sealed the rigid, thundering tool tight between his lips and deep into his mouth. He reveled in the taste and texture, the immensity of it, the spasms of pleasure he was eliciting from his servant. His own cock pulsed powerfully from within his trousers. He moved his head back and forth, sucking Kinnaird all the while.

Kinnaird dared to thrust his fingers into Duffield's thick hair, to take hold of the man's head. He pumped his hips to match the suctioning action of Duffield's mouth on his cock. The standing man's erection glided almost full length in and out of the kneeling man's face, his cock gleaming, glistening, swelling still more. The two men gasped air through their flared nostrils, the one gritting his teeth and staring down, the other gulping cock and intently staring up.

Kinnaird finally broke the well-oiled sexual machinery, pulling his spoke out of Duffield's sucking mouth—and just in time, too. "Would you like to have sexual intercourse with me, my Lord?" he asked, slyly. "In the chauffeur's hole?" Duffield hastily swallowed salty spunk as he nodded his head up and down. Kinnaird helped the man to his feet, then lay back on the bed. He lifted his legs and spread his buttocks with his hands. Duffield quickly unfastened his trousers and dropped them and his drawers, gazing into the winking pink eye of Kinnaird's asshole.

Duffield's cock was a steely, stretched length of swollen flesh and veins, sniffing high in the air for anus. The master gripped his cock, greasing it with the jar of oil Kinnaird happened to have handy. Then the older man blew out his moustache and clenched his teeth, steaming his shining cockhead up against the blossomed pucker of Kinnaird's ass.

Duffield's hood hit home, burst through, ballooning Kinnaird's ass ring. Both men shuddered, Kinnaird's cheeks and Duffield's legs quivering. Duffield drove into the man's ass with his cock, the master in the driver's seat now, plunging deep into Kinnaird's hole, until his balls touched up against the other man's buttocks, his huge cock lodged entirely in the hot, tight confines of Kinnaird's chute.

Both men sighed, heavily. Duffield gripped Kinnaird's lean thighs to his chest, rutting his buried, burning cock around in the man's superheated hole. Kinnaird grasped his own straining erection and pumped it.

"Fuck my ass, my Lord!" he pleaded. "Please, fuck me hard!"

It was harpy's-chord music to Duffield's glowing ears. He thrust slowly back and forth, easing his cock in and out of Kinnaird's gripping ass. Then he pumped faster, harder, sweat beetling his high brow, his damp hands slipping on Kinnaird's quaking thighs while he pounded his cock into the man's ass. Kinnaird pumped his cock all the while, just as fast and hard, pulling on his nipples as he did so, the muscles on his arms and chest clenching, his buttocks and body rocking to the cocking beat of Duffield's impassioned fucking.

"Let me…! Let me…jack you!" Lord Duffield yelped, pumping into Kinnaird's ass with furious intensity. He brushed Kinnaird's hand aside and grasped the man's surging cock, wildly pumping it. His thighs cracked Kinnaird's cheeks, his chute-churning cock cleaving the man almost in two.

Kinnaird craned his neck and clutched both his nipples, his body shunting and balls flapping, his cock frantically jerked by the man lodged inside his ass. Then he shouted and spasmed, the frantic erotic stroking too much for him. A rope of hot semen shot out of his clenched cock, followed by another, and another, while Duffield fisted the jumping member and fucked Kinnaird to a frenzy.

Suddenly, Duffield jerked and roared, his own squeezed appendage erupting in Kinnaird's convulsing chute. He splashed sizzling sperm against Kinnaird's bowels, splatted it home with the hammering tip of his spear, again and again and again.

The two men came in a mad rush and a gush of semen and emotion, joined as one in ecstasy at the meeting of cock and ass.

Lord Duffield had hardly pulled out of Robert Kinnaird's gaping chute, when the chauffeur shrewdly stated, "I guess I'll be getting it regularly from both ends now, my Lord." He held out his hand, a grin of avarice on his sensuous lips, his asshole now leaking come onto the sheets below.

"So that's your game, is it?" Duffield responded, giving his gleaming cock a rough shake. "I've had a detective watching you, Kinnaird, as I'm sure you're aware."

Kinnaird nodded, still smiling.

"And I had his agency fully investigate you as well."

Kinnaird frowned, his asshole puckering.

"You're wanted for 'passing the queer,' I believe they call it—dealing in counterfeit currency in London, posing as one Richard Burns." Lord Duffield smiled, grimly. "So, no, there will be no more blackmail here, Kinnaird. If you choose to tell your scandalous story to the newspapers—about your dealings with her Ladyship and myself—I'll have no choice but to tell the police of your whereabouts. On the other hand, if you agree to take a back passage to India, I'll ensure you a position at one of my plantations there, and, suffice it to say, I'll come 'visit' you from time to time—with special favors, of course."

The two men glared at each other.

With a sigh, Robert Kinnaird squirmed off the bed and sunk to his knees on the floor, dutifully tucking his master's cock into his trousers before buttoning the tweed back up. Only then did the two men regard each other with mutual satisfaction once again.

# MASTER JEFFY LEARNS A LESSON

## Sasha Payne

The starlight was smothered in the fog-filled sky. As a cock crowed, the day began in the house. Bedclothes were pulled back or thrown off. Feet were plunged into worn slippers and shoulders into threadbare gowns. Doors were cracked open as servants estimated their chances of returning to their own rooms without being seen.

Downstairs, in the family quarters, Lord Arthur protested sleepily as the bedclothes were pulled back.

"It's the middle of the night," he complained.

"It's six a.m."

"That's what I said, come back to bed," Lord Arthur ordered. He opened one eye as warm lips kissed his cheek. "I'll make it worth your while."

"Go back to sleep, your Lordship."

In the kitchen, Mrs. Beaker put her hands on her hips.

"Remember now, young Stephen, you don't pester his Lordship. You take the tray in, open the curtains and leave."

"Perhaps I should see to his Lordship?" James offered. He was a tall man, slim but muscular. He took pains to be beautifully turned out. His chestnut hair was always perfect and his uniform crisp.

"And then what?" asked Mrs. Beaker. "Send Stephen up to the honorable Bertie?"

Stephen's eyes widened as he clutched the breakfast tray to his chest.

"No, no, naturally not," James said. "Stephen, you are locking your door at night, aren't you?"

"Oh yes, Mr. Cummings!"

"Has anyone been rattling your handle?" Mrs. Beaker demanded.

Stephen looked uncertain. He was the boot boy, the most junior member of the staff, and only three years out of the orphanage.

"Rattling the handle of your bedroom door," James further explained.

"Oh, not more than once or twice a night, Mr. Cummings," Stephen promised.

Mrs. Beaker sighed and looked at James. "Have a word with Mr. Bertie would you?"

"He's unlikely to listen to me."

Mrs. Beaker nudged him with her elbow. "Ask him nicely then."

James took a breath as he opened the door to the honorable Bertie's bedroom. There was the usual trap of tangled underwear strewn on the floor. In any other household, Bertie would have his own valet, but Lord Arthur grew irritated with constantly having to pay them off when they grew bored of Bertie's busy hands.

"Who's there?" Bertie muttered as James put down the breakfast tray.

"James, Mr. Bertie," he said.

"Not little Stephen?" Bertie asked plaintively. "He has the most adorable little…"

"His Lordship has been most explicit on the subject," James said severely as he poured Bertie a cup of tea.

"Oh, has he! Oh, has he indeed!" Bertie brushed his dark hair out of his eyes and smoothed his beard with his fingers. He was a large man, tall and heavyset, but with curiously delicate fingers and a light step that had surprised many an unwary boot boy and footman. "It's the hypocrisy that annoys me, James; it is fine and good for him to carry on, but if I show a bit of…interest then I get a ten minute lecture on duty and not harassing the servants." Bertie tucked into his scrambled eggs. "I'm surprised he even lets you in here."

"I believe his Lordship considers me capable of expressing any disinterest in an appropriate manner," James calmly stated.

Bertie sighed. "He smells of cheap soap and hair oil, and last week at dinner there was a tiny bit of shaving foam just under his ear."

"Stephen?"

"Of course, Stephen. I didn't mean Arthur did I? I could have licked it off. I could have thrown him onto the dining table and ripped off all my clothes and all his clothes! We could have made wild passionate love on top of the mashed potatoes and asparagus!"

James gently pushed Bertie back into bed. "Perhaps less pepper in the future, sir?"

"I don't care about bally pepper! I'm a red-blooded man, James, and I need a man! It was so much easier when I was at school; everywhere you looked there were chimney sweeps, gardener's boys, and kitchen boys with their rough hands and dirty faces. Oh James, kiss me!"

The tray went crashing to the floor as Bertie embraced James and kissed him.

"Oh, you smell of cheap cologne!" he cried rapturously.

"It was a present from his Lordship," James protested.

"Yes, he's always been parsimonious." Bertie heaved his nightshirt over his head and cast it away as James's fingers danced over his own buttons. "Tear them off! Cast them aside!"

"I only have three sets," James said as he put his clothes aside.

"If you were my man I'd have you wearing clothes that tear away at a touch."

"Those would be very difficult to keep clean," James made note as he slipped between the sheets.

"To hell with keeping the damned things clean." Bertie crushed his lips against James's. "I wish the whole bally house could see us."

"They'll probably hear us just the same," James said as he slid down the bed.

"I hope they do." Bertie pushed his fingers through James's hair as the footman pushed his face into Bertie's nest of neat pubic hair. "I hope they hear us at the bally train station!" Bertie gasped as James took his length into his mouth.

Bertie's fingers slipped and slid in James's hair as they fought for purchase. James's hands gripped the other man's meaty thighs as he held Bertie down and played him like an instrument: a soft breath there, a gentle press here, and a long gliding lick following a series of sweet sucks.

"Jiminy Cricket!" Bertie bellowed as his testicles rose.

James continued holding him down as he played to the end, drawing Bertie to the crescendo before allowing him to fall back against the pillow.

"Golly," Bertie said indistinctly as James discretely visited the hand basin. "That was the best one yet."

"Thank you, Mr. Bertie," James gravely replied as he dressed.

"Aren't you staying 'til I bowl for your wicket?"

James smiled ever so slightly. "No, thank you, sir, not this morning."

Bertie lent up on his elbow. "Aha! Saving it up for Jeffy!"

"I beg your pardon, sir! I don't know what you mean!"

Bertie laughed. "There's no point in you pretending. Everyone knows he sends you into a fizz. Don't know what you see in him, really. Rich boys are frightfully boring. Find a nice, strong gardener or sailor, that's my advice. Someone big and manly."

James restrained a sigh. "Someone who smells of cheap aftershave and has calloused hands?" he suggested.

"That's the ticket," Bertie eagerly agreed.

"About young Stephen," James began, "he's very sheltered."

Bertie pouted. "No rattling his door handle?"

"Or knocking on his door either."

It was a beautiful day in early July. The sky was bright blue, the birds were singing and George Holm, gentleman about town, was blissfully sore from a thorough rogering he'd received the night before—rogering, petering and, he seemed to remember, a pretty decent dicking.

Atkins was not amused. He loomed at the end of George's bed like the angel of death, or at least a cherub of spanked botties.

"Time to get up is it?" George asked weakly. The only problem with late nights was the morning after. George tried to avoid mornings whenever possible. Unpleasant things. Nothing good came from them.

"Indeed, sir," Atkins intoned. George risked a glance and wished he hadn't. Atkins was a splendid chap in innumerable ways and extremely understanding of George's little foibles. But last night he'd been called away from his club because George hadn't been able to apply key to door with anything resembling precision.

"Strong drink is a mocker," George groaned. He looked at the cup that Atkins held out to him. "What is this?"

"A strong drink, sir," Atkins dryly retorted.

"Ha ha...ooh." George gingerly sat up in bed. "Those boys didn't half play rough last night."

Atkins raised an eyebrow as George busied himself with the cup of strong coffee.

If Atkins was refusing to enjoy tales of George's misadventures then he must be truly annoyed, thought the master. Retribution, George was sure, would be firm and merciless, much like Atkins himself.

George looked at his valet over the rim of his cup. He was both taller and broader than George was, with a placid old-fashioned sort of face: square of jaw and deep set of eyes. He also had shoulders like a bull and hands like ham hocks—though Atkins's shoulders were not his only body part that resembled a bull.

George finished his coffee and handed it to Atkins. "Much on the old agenda today?"

"Indeed, sir; the house party, in fact."

"Oh crumbs! Is that today? I'm in no fit state to be tramping the countryside. Aunt Lolly is always trying to marry me off and all. Anyone would think I was some princess being shipped off to a harem," George grumbled.

Atkins's mouth twitched. It wasn't anything as vulgar as a smile, but it was a start. And then he yanked the bedclothes from the bed and unceremoniously dumped George onto the floor.

"I say!" George protested.

"I have taken the liberty of packing for the weekend, sir, and the car is ready, unless the train is to be preferred?"

There was the tiniest hint of pleading in Atkins's voice. After all, he hated riding in George's car. For a moment George considered the train, but the blighter had just thrown him onto the floor.

"The car it is," he stated.

Atkins gave a tiny sigh as he folded up the sheets. "Yes, sir."

"What are you doing?"

"Preparing to send the linens for laundering, sir," Atkins replied, reminding George once more of his ability to make 'sir' sound like an insult.

"Right now?"

"Yes, sir. Your aunt is waiting in the lounge. The honorable Honoria."

"Tell her I'm in bed."

Atkins swept toward the door bearing the bedclothes in his arms. "Alas, sir, she is unlikely to believe it when she sees I am sending out the linens."

George looked around the room. "Where are my clothes?"

"Packed, sir," Atkins informed as he disappeared into the hallway.

"Ha bally ha!"

This was not Atkins's revenge; it was too simple. This was merely another battle in his war to make George wake up in the morning. Atkins loved mornings, but he would of course.

In any case, Aunt Honoria looked George up and down when he walked into the room.

"You are naked."

"No I'm not. I'm wearing slippers."

"Nowhere that they would help. I hope you're not going eccentric on us. Your Uncle Bertie is quite bad enough," she said.

"Atkins has packed for our house party. All the clothes he hasn't packed he's sent to be laundered," George explained.

"So you have upset him somehow. I don't know why he puts up with you."

"Hang on a dashed minute; I'm the one naked here," George protested.

"You are an empty-headed ass who spends most of his time either drinking with or betting against his equally asinine friends. Atkins, suffice it to say, is a treasure."

Atkins materialized as if summoned forth by the god of servants. "Thank you, your Ladyship."

"Do be a darling, Atkins, and give my useless lump of a nephew some clothes," Honoria requested. "Objectively attractive is still subjectively unappealing when the subject is one's own nephew."

Atkins inclined his head politely. "Indeed, Lady Honoria," he agreed.

George whistled as Atkins loaded up the car with bags. It was a desperately cheerful whistle, the sort of whistle that a man made when he knew that punishment would not be long in coming. For now, he could enjoy the way the muscles in Atkins's arms flexed as he worked. In turn, Atkins grunted a little as he carried the heavy bags, a sound he often made when he was exerting himself. It was a sound George had grown quite to appreciate.

Atkins finished packing the car and carefully straightened his sleeves. He held open the car door for George and waited patiently.

"Thank you, Atkins," George said as he climbed into the car. He waited until Atkins walked around to the passenger side and climbed in. "I say, Atkins, some of those cases looked jolly heavy."

"Indeed, sir, it pays to be prepared when traveling."

"They're all uh...they're all clothes are they?" George asked.

The car zipped around a corner, sending a spray of dust madly dancing. Atkins grasped his hat with both hands.

"There are clothes, sir, shoes, some lotions and scents," Atkins replied.

"Is uh...is that all?" George asked tentatively.

"I have brought such necessaries and implements as may be required," Atkins somberly replied.

"Golly."

Stephen, furiously polishing the silverware, looked up at the sound of Chesterton's heavy tread upon the step.

"Oh, still here with us are you?" James said as the door opened and the butler walked in. "I wondered if you left in the night."

"I don't answer to you," Chesterton said. He was older than James, a stocky Welshman with a mane of silvery hair and a roman nose. He carried himself with a little less ease and a little more dignity than he had in years gone by, but he was still a powerfully built man.

"We've done the trays," Stephen offered. "I took up his Lordship's tray."

Chesterton nodded as he strolled across the kitchen. "Never any problems with his Lordship."

"He was awake when I got up there," Stephen said, "The room was a right mess. It looked like the sheets had been pulled out of the bed and everything."

"Mind your manners," James said and cuffed Stephen's ear.

\* \* \*

The car was approaching the manor at a decent clip when George spotted the other car lumbering along.

"Dear God," George said, "That's Aunt Lolly and her mob; I'd know their wagon train anywhere."

"Master Jeffy will be pleased," Atkins observed.

"What? Oh because of James? Blast Jeffy and Lolly and the lot of them. I hate house parties. As soon as they spot us we'll all have to pull over, and Aunt Lolly will insist on cousin Kitty riding in here. If we don't pull over then I will never hear the end of it."

Atkins considered the situation for a moment.

"Might I suggest, sir, pulling over before the car is seen? The woods here are reasonably pleasant and very quiet. It's unlikely we would be disturbed, and we would still arrive before luncheon."

George grinned mischievously. "I say, Atkins, what would we be doing while we waited?"

"We could commune with nature, sir," Atkins replied.

"Whizzer!" said George, and sharply pulled the car over.

He hopped out and began scouting for a secluded spot as Atkins slid out of his seat and gracefully removed his hat and coat. Atkins placed them carefully on the seat and considered his belt: it was supple calfskin, a Christmas present from George. It would be both sufficient and appropriate. Atkins then followed George into the woods.

The trees were thickly clustered here and the noise of the road had been cushioned by the murmuring of the oaks and the buzzing of the bees. A canopy of branches overhead turned the brilliant sunshine into a soft haze as a single bird flew overhead, the waft of its wings making the leaves quiver.

"Beautiful here, don't you think?" George asked, almost in a whisper. He was leaning back against a tree, feeling the bark beneath his fingers. All the trees here were strong, thick and tall. Old trees living in the midst of flowers and moss.

"Yes it is," Atkins replied. He rolled up his sleeves neatly and loosened his tie.

"Do you think it's always this quiet?" George again whispered as Atkins prowled ever closer.

"No."

"No?"

"This is the wilds, sir; animals live here," Atkins said, "and where animals live, animals fight, and die and..."

George, his eyes staring and enormous, saturated with darkness and lust said, "And?"

"And fuck."

George shivered in delight at the forbidden wickedness of the word, at the harsh, short consonants and vowels uttered in Atkins's meticulous tones.

"Is that what they do?" George loosened his own tie as Atkins leant over him, pinning him against the tree. He closed his eyes as Atkins crushed his mouth against his own. *Kiss* was too meek and mild a word, too delicate for a man like Atkins or the things he did. Atkins then insinuated a hand down George's trousers and took easy possession of him, while George squeaked, soft and helpless, as his hands found the knotted muscles of the other man's arm.

Atkins pulled his hand free, making George moan, and promptly removed his belt. He took a half step back. George watched him with heavy-lidded eyes.

"Undress," Atkins commanded, and George licked his lips.

"Here?"

"Yes."

"In the woods?"

"Yes."

"Where anyone might see?" George asked, wide eyed.

The ghost of a smile touched Atkins's lips.

"Yes. Now. No more talking," he commanded.

George tugged off his tie and yanked off his jacket, then squirmed out of his shirt, kicked off his shoes, and slipped off his socks. Atkins piled them all carefully in the shadow of an oak tree. Lastly, George tentatively removed his shorts and handed them over.

"On the ground, sir, on your hands and knees."

George gulped and shimmied down onto the ground. He made himself comfy on all fours with his legs spread wide. He heard the rustle of leaves as Atkins moved closer and then felt the caress of the valet's rough skin as Atkins drew his fingers down his spine. George shivered in delight but didn't raise his head. He didn't need to look over his shoulder to know that Atkins was standing behind him, that those huge hands were opening the little pot that resided in the inner pocket of his coat. He shivered again when Atkins placed the pot on his buttocks and left it sitting there as if on a shelf. From the rustling, George knew that Atkins was lowering his trousers and drawers, and he listened to the light breath so close and felt the warm heat emanating from the other man's bare flesh—in fact, they filled George's awareness. Nothing existed but the leaves underneath his hands and knees, the trees around them, the duet of their breathing and the rough skin of Atkins's hands as he grasped George's hips.

"Sir was generous with his affections last night," Atkins observed. "Such jolly fun."

"Too generous?" George asked.

Atkins tutted. "Sir forgets he was told not to talk." He pushed his belt between George's teeth and buckled it behind his head.

George gnashed the leather between his teeth and closed

his eyes. He mewed when Atkins again gripped his hips and he pushed back against Atkins's slow, deliberate thrusts. He tasted leather as he bit down and closed his eyes. His own breath was getting deeper as his fingers clutched the grass and flowers. George heard Atkins's little grunt as he deepened his thrusts. George was already close. He shifted his weight to his left hand, and the world paused, waiting for a moment as he lifted his right. Atkins chuckled and continued as he was; if George fell, then he fell. George's arm shook for a moment but then his fingers slipped around his shaft. He felt their breathing, heard their heartbeats, smelt sweat and summer.

George came first, gasping his release into the grass and nearly overbalancing. He tumbled onto his elbows, face into the wildflowers, and groaned in pleasured pain as Atkins thrust in ever deeper. Atkins's fingers squeezed his hips tightly, branding George with bruises before he finally came. They panted together until the world cleared, and then George rolled away to lie on his back.

"Whizzer," he murmured.

James checked his hair for the sixth time. Behind him, Chesterton shook his head as he inspected the silverware.

"Give over, you'll make it fall out if you keep fussing with it like that."

"Some of us take pride in our appearance and wish to give the house a good name," James retorted.

"Is that what you call it when you're flapping around waiting for Mr. Jeffy to make a grand entrance? He'll do you no good, James. That lad is not to be trusted. We both know the sort."

"I don't know what you mean," James said.

"Pity; everyone else knows exactly what I mean," Chesterton retorted.

"He's just...he's just young and confused. That's all."

Chesterton began packing up the silverware. "He's hardly that young. Older than Master George, and nobody ever accused him of being confused. Well, not about what he wanted."

"Not about that, no," James snorted. "Plenty else!"

"But not that."

On the wall, one of the bells began jangling. They both turned to look at it. Chesterton put on his coat as James fled for the door.

"It's the front door," Chesterton chided. "I'm still the butler here."

"Yes, but..."

Chesterton raised his eyebrows. "You're going to get burnt, James. Trust me on this one."

"Blast," George said as the car approached the manor. "They must have stopped off for a picnic or something; they're only just ahead of us."

As George parked the car, the family members were just clambering out of their car. Kitty was a pretty girl but had no sense of humor—a capital offense in George's opinion—and took everything far too seriously. A person oughtn't to be found wanting if he went to breakfast without a tie, in George's opinion.

"Master Jeffy has not brought a valet," Atkins observed.

"You keep your mitts off Master Jeffy."

A flicker of amusement threaded Atkins's face and then promptly dissolved. "Indeed, sir. James would be most put out."

George got out of the car as Atkins slid across to the driving seat.

"He'll go bald," George said.

"Sir?"

"Jeffy," George said. "Those fluffy blond types always do."

"George! Stop standing around like a nincompoop. Come over here at once!"

"I daren't look. Is it Aunt Lolly?" George asked, shoulders scrunched.

"Alas, yes, sir," Atkins said, then gunned the engine and peeled out, taking the car around to the servant's entrance.

George sighed and with a heavy heart turned and tramped over to his relatives. Jeffy was complaining as usual.

"I want James to be my valet," he said. "I don't want any damned boot boy!"

Chesterton the butler gave George a look that suggested the argument had been proceeding for some time. "James takes care of Mr. Bertie," Chesterton said.

"I just bet he does!"

"Stephen is quite capable, sir."

"Oh don't be such a bore, Jeffy," George said. "Chesterton has better things to do than listen to you whine! Let him get on with his job."

Chesterton gave George a slight nod, while Jeffy reddened.

At that moment, Arthur wandered out and exchanged pleasantries.

"Chesterton won't let James be my valet," Jeffy complained. "He's attempting to palm me off with the boot boy. The boot boy! I expect a footman as my valet at the very least."

"Well..." Arthur wavered.

"Sort it out," Lolly snapped. "Jeffy wants James, not some half-trained delinquent orphan brat."

"Oh, well, fine, sort it out, Chesterton," Arthur said, waving a hand.

\* \* \*

"How unfortunate," Atkins said when George gave him the gossip.

"Rather!" said George. "Chesterton looked like he was plotting a grisly death. Uncle Arthur best watch his back."

"A wise servant expects no loyalty from his master." Atkins brushed George's suit with a clothes brush. They were getting ready for lunch, and their clothes, among other things, had been dirtied by the journey.

"Tiny bit harsh!" George protested. "Chesterton's been here for years. He deserves some consideration. Not to mention Uncle Arthur and him..." Atkins raised an eyebrow. "Don't give me that look. You know as well as I do that Uncle Arthur and Chesterton are, well, Uncle Arthur and Chesterton."

"Indeed, sir."

Luncheon was a tense affair, not aided by George being seated opposite Kitty. Things did not improve.

"It is past time you married," Uncle Arthur announced. "Lolly and Honoria have been extremely clear, often enough, and I am fed up of hearing about it."

"Who d'you mean?" Jeffy demanded.

"You, and George, and Kitty," Arthur said. "You're all too old to be spending your time at clubs and causes."

"I can't marry Jeffy and Kitty," George protested, "and they can hardly marry one another."

"Do be sensible for once in your fat-headed life," Lolly said. "You'll marry Kitty. She can get some sense into you."

"I will not," he said.

"Do not talk to back to me! I say you will," she replied.

"Don't I get a bally say?" George demanded.

"First we'll get rid of your club," Kitty said. "It's entirely frivolous."

"I like frivolous!"

"Then," Kitty said, ignoring him, "we'll be living with mummy and daddy at Ravenhurst, so you won't need your valet."

"You don't deserve him anyway," Lolly said.

George looked up at Atkins, registering the look in his eye, and merely scowled at his relatives.

"What are we going to do?" George asked as he changed for golf. He had complete faith in Atkins's ability to deal with any emergency.

"Sir refers to his intended marriage to Miss Kitty."

"Yes, yes, obviously. I'm sure you have your giant brain devoted to the task."

Atkins knelt down to lace up George's golf shoes. "Perhaps it would be best if Miss Kitty were to deem you unsuitable marriage material?" he suggested.

"I thought everyone already knew that," George replied.

"Something more extreme will likely be required, sir."

George shivered. "I'm going to really regret this, aren't I?" he said. "All because I was too squiffy to unlock the door, and you got called away from your club."

Atkins stood and brushed off his trousers. "If that was indeed the case, sir, I might draw sir's attention to the fact that he visits his club three or four times a week, while I am only able to visit my club once a month."

George winced. "When you put it that way, then I suppose it was pretty stiff."

Atkins straightened George's tie and picked up the golf bag.

"Shall we proceed downstairs for your pregame drinks, sir?"

"Lead the way, Atkins," George said sadly. "I'll follow and consider my certain doom."

"Very good, sir."

"Are my trousers too tight, James?" Jeffy asked. He was standing in the middle of the room, shirtless, and wearing very tight golf trousers that clung to his bottom, thighs and calves. He was an amateur boxer, and it showed in his build. Muscles bulged in his chest, arms, and legs, but he still moved like an athlete more than a hired bruiser. In fact, he could have modeled for Atlas or navy recruiting posters.

"I wouldn't wish to say," James muttered.

"Come and feel," Jeffy said. He was smirking as he posed for the footman. "Run your hand along my legs and tell me if you find anything notable."

James, already uncomfortable, flushed bright red. "You're going to be late to the game, sir."

"It's a dreadful bore." Jeffy put on his shirt and tie. "I bet you and I could find lots of other ways to pass the time."

"I don't know what you mean, sir!"

"Oh, we both know you do." Jeffy pulled James close and gazed into his eyes. He leant in until James closed said eyes. "Now go and fetch my clubs; they're downstairs," he ordered. "Go on! You didn't actually think I was going to kiss you? You're far too wet. Run along."

James gritted his teeth as he left the room and stamped downstairs. Chesterton and Atkins were waiting for Arthur and George to emerge from their pregame drinks.

"What's the matter with you?" Chesterton asked.

"Mr. Jeffy," James snapped as he grabbed the clubs. "He laughed at me! He made me think...and then he laughed at me. Don't you dare say you told me so. Don't you dare."

"He needs taking down a peg or two," Chesterton said. "Arguing over his valet. Making demands. Laughing at you. It's not on. Your master never treats you like that, does he, Mr. Atkins?"

"Mr. George has his foibles," Atkins said thoughtfully, "however, a lack of respect is not one of them. I understand who pays the wages; he understands who decides if he will sleep alone."

"How do you do that?" James asked.

"You try too hard. You go running after him," Chesterton said.

"I won't do that again. Nobody does that to me," James replied.

"Let me think about it," Chesterton said. "Whatever else, he needs to learn a lesson."

There were birds chirping as the balls were cupped, dropped, and then kissed by the golf clubs.

"Things a bit tense, what?" George remarked as he and Atkins entered a wooded copse in search of a stray ball. "I know Chesterton is narked with Uncle Arthur, but what's bitten James's biscuit?"

"Mr. Jeffy," Atkins informed him.

"What? He didn't actually bite him did he? I know he's a bounder but biting without invitation would be beyond the pale."

"No, sir, far worse: he laughed at James," Atkins said.

George squeezed his eyes shut. "Oh gosh! What a thing to do! Why are you telling me this?"

Atkins shrugged. "In the event of a settling of score, your assistance might be invaluable, sir."

"Oh revenge! Rather. James can count on me. Jeffy, after all, is an absolute rotter."

"Indeed, sir." Atkins indicated the ball.

"Oh," George said, looking at the position, "dash it."

"Might I suggest an alternative pastime?" Atkins said.

"What did you have in that throbbing mind of yours?"

Atkins pushed George against an oak tree and then turned him to face it.

"I say, Atkins, this seems a might...risky," George said doubtfully.

"Indeed, sir," Atkins agreed. He wrapped George's arms around the tree and walked around it. Atkins tied George's wrists together with sturdy twine before kneeling to tie his ankles together.

"Um, Atkins, I don't want to wreck the mood or anything but Uncle Arthur was jolly close behind us and Kitty was hard at his heels." His voice rose sharply as Atkins pulled George's trousers and drawers down around his knees. "I have to wonder if this is quite a first-rate notion?"

"That would depend on the intended outcome, sir," Atkins said. He took three clean golf balls and wrapped them in a handkerchief.

George's eyes widened. "Atkins! You can't leave me here for Uncle Arthur or Kitty to find!"

Atkins pushed the golf balls and the handkerchief inside George's mouth and tied the ends behind the back of George's head, then blindfolded George with another handkerchief.

"I am quite confident, sir, that Miss Kitty will not consider you marriageable after this, and that you will drink less on my next club night." He gave George a little pat on the rump before he left.

George kept very quiet. It was not a thing that came naturally for him, and neither was cogitation. Yet he was hopeful that if he was quiet the others might pass right by without seeing him.

So he waited. Then after far too short an interval, he heard a heavy tread. Not Kitty then and probably not the boot boy carrying her clubs; he'd have fainted, after all, the minute he saw George there, tied like a Christmas goose. The heavy steps came very close. George mumbled through the gag and squirmed in his bonds. A heavy hand rested on his waist and he felt warm breath on his cheek as the other hand untied his blindfold.

It was Chesterton! George could have gladly kissed him most days, but at that moment he would have started with the butler's feet.

"Pardon me for the interruption, Mr. George," Chesterton said, untying the gag, "I think it best to be sure in these situations. Would you wish to be untied?"

"Yes! Dear God, please untie me, Chesterton, and I will love you forever!"

"How did you come to be here, Mr. George?" Chesterton asked as he moved to untie George's wrists.

"Atkins thought it would make Kitty refuse to marry me," George replied. "He's also rather annoyed at me."

"I see," said Chesterton, kneeling down to untie George's feet. "Have you heard of this 'tattoo' that the Prince of Wales has indulged in? They have become quite the thing among the aristocracy."

"Um, yes, I believe so. Sort of a thing sailors do, isn't it?" George said, pulling up his drawers and trousers.

"Miss Kitty despises them," Atkins explained. "She would never marry a gentleman who had one."

"Does she? How wonderful to know! I will find a tattooist forthwith and select an appropriate design. I thank you again for your kindness and solicitude." George stretched his limbs and brushed his sleeves. "I must say, Chesterton, that this has been a pleasantly surprising interlude. I was quite concerned that if anyone found me, I should have to pay the piper for them to let me go, if you understand my meaning."

"I do," Chesterton said. "Not that it would be unpleasant to accept, but Lord Arthur would have been extremely unhappy."

"Gosh, he wouldn't have dismissed you would he?"

Chesterton considered it for a moment. "That is unlikely."

"I shouldn't worry overmuch about upsetting Uncle Arthur then," George said. "He rather has some sort of an upset coming after taking Jeffy's side against you, if you don't mind an observation."

"He would be unlikely to dismiss me, Mr. George, but he would very likely remove you from his will," Atkins said.

George bounced up on his tiptoes. "Seems to me then that Jeffy would be quite the spiffy person for Uncle Arthur to think that he was encroaching on his territory."

Chesterton crossed his hands across his stomach. "Mr. Atkins has been speaking out of school?"

"I wouldn't say that," George said quickly. "Particularly not where he might hear me."

Chesterton smiled. "Thank you for the advice, Mr. George."

"Thank you for the rescue!"

All too soon, George found Atkins tooling around the eighth hole. It was far enough away to disclaim responsibility for any scandal, but close enough to hear the perhaps inevitable fun when someone found George. If he was surprised to see George stride out of the undergrowth, then he covered it well.

"Good news, Atkins, a little bird has informed me that Kitty simply loathes tattoos. If I receive one then she will simply refuse to marry, even upon pain of fiery death."

"Indeed, sir?"

"Absolutely," George said. He kicked the heel of his foot

with the toe of his other foot. "I thought perhaps I'd have your initials tattooed upon me."

Atkins tenaciously fought a smile. "Might I enquire how you endeavored to free yourself?"

"Ah, I didn't," George admitted. "Some little birdy did rather trip over me as I was trussed to the tree. Terribly embarrassing of course."

"How worrisome."

"I don't believe it's about to become public knowledge." George waggled his eyebrows. "Besides, there's likely to be a much bigger scandal soon enough."

"Indeed, sir?" Atkins inquired.

George bounced up on his toes. "I rather hope so. I gave him a jolly good idea, and I'd hate for it to go to waste."

The house was dark and the only light was from the moon and the stars as they shone through the windows. The honorable Bertie hissed and cursed under his breath as the narrow stairs to the servant's quarters creaked under his steps. There was no carpet, and the old, faded wallpaper was peeling from the walls. It was so raw and squalid that it made Bertie's blood fizz in his veins.

He approached Stephen's door and tried the handle. No luck, it was locked again. Bertie gave it a forlorn little rattle and was about to creep away when he heard a muffled moan—a moan and then a squeak. Bertie pressed his ear to the door and then his eye to the keyhole. It was dark in the room and all he could hear was Stephen's sleeping breath. There was another moan and a jangle of bedsprings. Bertie stood up and tiptoed along the corridor, listening for the soft sounds.

At this room, the moaning was more muffled words, and a light shone through the keyhole. Bertie pressed his eye to the keyhole, the unlocked door suddenly swinging open.

Across the house, George awoke to the sound of screaming and a good deal of yelling. He tiptoed out of the bedroom and out onto the main staircase, where he found Kitty glowering at the assembled staff, while Bertie made cow eyes at Stephen.

"What's going on?" George asked.

"The honorable Bertie caught Mr. Jeffy in Mr. Chesterton's room!" Stephen erupted. "And he was all tied up! And naked. Naked! And gagged!"

"Stop saying that!" Kitty snapped.

"If you're going to behave like a child, then you can go back to bed," James said sharply.

"Golly," said George as Lolly marched down the stairs, dragging Jeffy behind her by the ear. "Was Mr. Chesterton there?"

"Mr. Chesterton was not there; he and I were in my room playing cards. He had no idea that Mr. Jeffy was there," James said, with only the merest quaver in his voice.

"Well then," George said, "all's well that ends well. Good night all."

And that, thank goodness, was that!

# BOHEMIAN
# RHAPSODY

## Rob Rosen

The bell chimed just as my head hit the pillow. It was quite late already, too late for a visitor. The lady and gentleman of the house, my employers, were both long fast asleep, so it couldn't have been them. Was it one of the staff, somehow locked outside? Perhaps, but it seemed highly unlikely and equally improper that they'd be ringing the front bell and not the one at the servant's entrance. Still, it had rung from the front, and was still chiming even as I reluctantly flung myself out of bed, covered myself up with a proper robe and trudged up the stairs, yawning and grumbling all the while.

"Stop that blasted ringing!" I shouted. The ringing promptly stopped and was replaced by a rather loud knocking. I sighed as I pried the door open and stared angrily through the gap. "That's not what I meant for you to do, sir."

He grinned and doffed his flaming-red bowler hat. "Apologies, my good man," he replied. "I thought to yodel, but deemed it unlikely that anyone but a goat would respond."

I coughed as he righted himself. Aside from the bowler, crimson as it was, he was dressed in nothing of the clothes of the day. Not a suit, at least not a fashionable one, nor even a jacket or a tie; in their place he wore baggy britches of a greenish hue and a blousy shirt made of some sort of tanned hide. His hair was long rather than short, his beard scraggly and pointed, his moustache oddly limp and bushy. Had it not been for his stunningly blue eyes, which seemed to shimmer in the moonlight, I might have slammed the door in his face and returned with a pistol. Instead, I inquired, "Do you have business here, sir? It is, in case you hadn't realized, rather late."

His grin widened as he looked up at the stars, then back my way before replying, "Must be early enough somewhere though, I'd imagine."

I nodded as his eyes stayed locked with my own, a tremor suddenly rippling beneath the center of my robe. Again I coughed. "In any case, as to my question..."

His nod mirrored my own. "Ah, yes. Business." He pointed down to his banged-up luggage and at an odd, wooden rectangular case by his feet, then produced a calling card. "George Emerson," he informed me, with a low bow. "And, yes, I do believe that I am a trifle late."

It was then, as I fought to remember if the master had informed me of an invited guest in his long litany of things I was to remember on a daily basis, that the gentleman in question presented himself.

His voice boomed from the stairwell behind where I was standing. "James!" he bellowed down at me. "Who is this... this...*Bohemian?*"

My face reddened. To answer my employer that I hadn't the foggiest notion of whom this, as he put it, *Bohemian* was, would not have been prudent. So instead I merely replied,

"George Emerson, sir. He's, um, he's..."

"Late," barked George, storming past me, luggage and case now in tow. "My apologies, sir. It was unavoidable, you see. The light this afternoon was deplorable, but this evening's dusk was, as the French say, *parfait*."

My master stood on the stairwell, transfixed, jaw hanging limp. This stranger's rapturous voice and oddly handsome looks, I quickly realized, had a way of doing this to a man—present company included. "Perfect," I intoned, gazing up the stairs. "He means perfect, sir."

My master, Byron Theodore, grimaced at my insolence, but then, heavens be praised, smiled and trotted down the stairs, his hand held out in greeting. "James," he said to me, over his shoulder. "This is that artist fellow I was telling you about." I hadn't a clue what he was referring to but was quite accustomed to that by then. "He's here to paint my portrait."

Again I was in the dark. And, yet, I replied, "Right, your portrait, sir." Which explained the oddly shaped wooden case dangling from this stranger's mitt of a hairy hand. "So we were expecting him." It came out a statement despite it being a question.

Master Byron glared my way. "But of course, James." He then turned to the portraitist, their free hands still interlocked. "We were expecting him this very afternoon, in truth, but no bother; he's here now, and that's all that matters."

*Amen*, I thought to myself, that ripple in my crotch turning to a storming river. Well-trained butler that I was, I rushed to George's side and gathered his belongings. I then looked to my master for some direction.

"Take him to the spare room downstairs, James." He then released his grip from George's and smiled, proudly, clearly delighted at this man's presence. Again, him and me both, truth be told. Because, Bohemian or not, George had a certain something I couldn't quite put my finger on, eager as my finger now was to, well, *put.* "We'll get started first thing in the morning, George, if that's all right with you."

George nodded. "Light permitting."

"Quite," said my master.

And with that, we were off, the artist following me through the house and down to the servant's quarters. "The spare room—"

"Does not exist, sir." I dropped his things in the hallway outside my own room instead. "The master seems to have forgotten that he turned the spare room into a storage area for his lady's doll collection."

George chuckled. "She has a room for nothing but dolls?"

Sadly, I didn't join him with a chuckle of my own. "A secondary room for her less treasured *children*, as she puts it. The main collection is kept in the master bedroom, behind glass."

His chuckle repeated. "Where all good children are kept."

I nodded. "To quote the master, *quite.*" Then I paused before opening the door to my room. "But I have a spare bed in here. The dolls didn't need it, you see."

He patted my back and pushed his way past me. "I should say not, James."

I followed him in and promptly lit the gas lamp on the dresser. My heartbeat doubled in time as I watched him hop on the bed next to my own. I then dropped his things in the corner of the room and turned back his way. "Servant's bathroom is down the hall, sir. Feel free to freshen up if you like."

He shrugged and kicked off his well-worn boots and rolled off his grubby socks. "All I need is a bed and some sleep, James. Today's been a long one, tomorrow promising more of the same."

And then I watched in stunned amazement as he removed his odd-looking tunic and slid out of his equally odd-looking britches, his naked body suddenly spread out before me, hairy as a wolf and just as lean. "Um," I managed, trying and failing not to stare, "do you need to borrow a gown of some sort, sir?"

He laughed, finely etched belly rising and falling as he did so. "Why, James? Are we to attend a ball later on?"

I coughed and slowly removed my robe, hopping into bed before covering myself with the blanket, lest he see the obvious bulge in my rather flimsy sleeping garments. "A gown to sleep in, sir," I informed him, fighting to catch my ragged breath.

I turned his way just as he once again shrugged. "I was born naked, James, and, in case I die in my sleep, plan to leave this world that way." His head turned my way as I doused the light, the room and his hirsute body now cast in silver moon-glow.

I gulped. "Suit yourself, sir. Suit yourself."

He lay flat on his back, head propped up on a pillow as he stared at the ceiling, while I in turn stared at him—lucky ceiling, even luckier me. He ran his fingers through his dense matting of chest hair and again turned his face my way. "Master Byron, nice-looking man, wouldn't you say?" I paused, unsure just how to reply. "I mean that from a purely artistic point of view, of course. He'll make a fine portrait model."

I stifled a laugh. "If you were painting a horse's ass, sir." My face reddened. I'd clearly said too much. Should've been paying attention to my manners rather than my guest's exposed willie. "Just joking, of course, sir."

He leaned up on his elbow, his body now turned my way. "He fancies me, you know."

My eyes went wide. "Well, he wouldn't have hired you if you weren't the finest artist, sir."

His chuckle returned, as did the swelling beneath my blanket.

"Not that kind of fancying, James." He grabbed his crotch, cock held in his mitt. "I mean he wants, well, *this*." The chuckle repeated itself, thicker this time, raspier.

I pursed my lips, stifling back a chuckle of my own. "You're daft," I eventually told him. "The master is married." I left the happily out. In truth, the dolls had it better than my master did when it came to my lady.

"As if that ever stopped anyone before," he replied, hand stroking his dick.

"How...how do you know that he *fancies* you?"

George nodded and released his prick, which now hovered in the air at half-mast. "An artist knows, James. We're sensitive to such things. Besides, I practically had to wrench my hand free of his back there."

I gazed in rapt wonder as his prick stiffened and grew. "That's just his way, sir," I explained.

He nodded—him and his prick both. "Exactly, James. Exactly."

Again I paused, carefully measuring my words like so much flour for a cake. "And is it *your* way, sir?"

The pause stretched, the silence in the room nearly deafening, but still his prick stood at attention. "As an artist, dear James, I see beauty in all its many forms."

This time I didn't bother to stifle the chuckle. "Which is a rather nicer way of saying yes." And then I pointed at his rigid fifth limb. "Though I must admit, *that's* nicer by far."

He gave it a thwack that sent it reeling. "Suddenly, James, I don't find myself so tired." He reached his hand across the small gap that divided our beds and yanked at my blanket. It slid to the floor in a muffled thump. "Ah, I see we are not attending a ball tonight, but, by the looks of that tent, going camping instead."

I grinned and pointed at his midsection. "And by the looks of that fetching rod of yours, *fishing* as well."

He hopped out of bed and stood over me. Had I been dreaming, I might have thought a slender bear had somehow gotten inside my room, and one with a horse's cock at that. But this was no dream, pleasant as the image was. And then he bent down and grabbed the hem of my sleeping gown, which he promptly lifted up and over my head. "Ah," he said. "I see we both have ample rods to fish with."

My own rod throbbed. I grinned at him as I shook it to and then fro. "Perhaps some *spear* fishing would indeed be fun."

His face craned in farther my way, until those stunning orbs of blue were directly in front of my muddy brown ones. His lips touched down upon my own, soft as a cloud, enough to make cotton seem rough in comparison. Once his tongue was through dancing inside my mouth and his beard finished mopping my saliva-drenched chin, he finally replied, "Fun seems like such a gross understatement, James. Like saying that Michelangelo was simply a decent sculptor."

I nodded my agreement and watched with intent as he went from standing on the floor to standing on my bed, one foot on either side of me as he slowly squatted down, my bed creaking and groaning all the while—or perhaps it was simply me doing the groaning. "Though Michelangelo couldn't have carved anything half as lovely as you, sir."

His lilting chuckle pierced through my very heart as he spit into his hand to moisten both his tender chute and my rigid prick. "I think you missed your calling as a wordsmith, dear James." And then down he went, his hole soon engulfing the tip of my cock, the helmeted head buried inside of him as he threw his head back and moaned with abandon.

As for me, I lay there, rapturously watching as he sunk lower and lower down, taking my prick with him, until the moonlit shaft was nowhere to be seen and my balls were brushing up against his hairy cheeks. "I think I've caught a big one," I gasped, taking a hold of his thick prick, a slow, even stroke quickly administered to it.

"As have I," he rasped in reply, riding my cock as if it were a prized stallion, my body suddenly on fire as my crotch met his ass.

My pace quickened on his cock, matching the rhythm of my prick up his tight, puckered hole. When his meat was at its thickest and his balls had clearly risen, I shoved one last time, deep inside of him. His back arched as a mighty stream of viscous fluid spewed out, dousing my belly and chest before spilling to the sheet below. At that same moment, his hole clenched tightly around my prick, which also then exploded, filling him up with so much spunk that it soon seeped out of him, dripping down my balls a split second later.

He huffed while I puffed, our bodies still united as his eyes again locked on to my own. "Perhaps I should paint slowly tomorrow, dear James."

I grinned, my hand still stroking his wilting prick. "Take all the time you need, sir. The bed shall be here for you." I licked the salty, sweet spunk off my fingers. "As shall I, sir. As shall I."

Suffice it to say, the artist bunked with the butler that night, leaving me in the morning with nothing but a cryptic message in my ear: "Let us see if the master is as adept as the servant today, dear James."

He was gone before I could wipe the morning from my eyes—gone, that is, but certainly not forgotten.

And when I served the master and his portraitist in the study a mere hour later, it was the master's turn to whisper in my ear,

"Do not disturb us, James. I will ring for you if I need you."

That was that. I left them to their devices, shutting the door behind me with barely a click. Though, of course, a mere door is not nearly enough to prevent a butler such as myself to peek inside, if I so chose.

The mansion, in fact, was full of rooms the size of closets that the staff used to monitor its inhabitants. How else would we know when a cup of tea was running low or a fire needed a new log, all before the master or his lady could ask for such things? It wasn't spying, after all, so much as our duty.

Though, yes, that day it was indeed spying. But how else was I to see what George had up his leathery sleeve—or down his odd-looking, billowing britches?

And so I slid back the wooden slat, revealing the latticed screen in front of it. I could then see and hear inside, while they could not see me in return. So long as I remained quiet, which I'd grown quite adept at over my years of service there, then they could not hear me either.

The master was dressed in all his finery that morning, looking resplendent in his top hat and finely tailored suit, ivory-handled walking stick by his side. As for the artist, he was pacing this way and that, circling his model one way and returning the other.

"Hmm," said George, agonizing minutes into this routine.

"Hmm, what?" asked my master, smiling like a proud peacock all the while.

George scratched beneath his crimson hat. "I just can't seem to get a feel for you this morning, sir."

"A *feel*? What, pray tell, does that mean?" he asked.

It was George's turn to smile, causing my pants to suddenly bulge around the crotch. "This suit you're in..."

"It's the best money can buy."

George nodded. "But it hides the man inside. And because of that I won't be able to draw you properly I'm afraid, not just yet."

"Until you get this *feel* for me, as you mentioned?" asked my master. "So how, exactly, can I help?"

George paused, his fingers tugging at the tip of his scraggly beard. "Perhaps if I were to see the man beneath, to understand his form, I'd be able to better capture you on canvas." And before my master could interject, it was added, "This is how the famed Italians do it, you see."

I covered my mouth to stifle back the laugh. I knew that was enough to do it. The artist was as cunning as he was beautiful, I thought to myself, shocked, just the same, to witness my master suddenly start to undress, the smile on his face now stony, locked nervously in place.

To be sure, I'd seen Byron Theodore in his undergarments before, but as to what lay beneath those, I doubted even the good lady had witnessed all of him in anything but the moonlight of their bedroom. And now, here he was, naked as the day he was born, the top hat still there, now completely out of place.

I groaned despite myself. My master was as handsome as he was ruthless, but naked he was nothing short of stunning. I chalked it up to good county living—and ample doses of it, too. Even the good artist seemed taken aback by the glory that was my naked master.

"Well?" asked the model. "Is this more to your liking?" The smile rose northward on his face. Though, miraculously, it wasn't the only thing rising in that direction. My master stared down as his prick stared up and out. "Dear me, I don't suppose you can paint *that* into the portrait."

George shook his head, though his eyes never once blinked.

"You'd then have to toss it in the fireplace as opposed to hanging it above."

My master laughed, cock bouncing as he did so. "Well then, only one way to make it go down." He took his pole of a prick and shook it at George. "Perhaps I shall let you do the honors, sir."

The artist quickly sank to his knees. "Honored is the word, sir." And with that, the proffered prick disappeared down George's throat, while my own prick got popped out of my work pants. The master then pumped his cock in and out, thrusting his glorious ass into the face below. As for me, I gazed longingly on, stroking the come up from my swaying balls.

It didn't take long—for either of us. All too soon, the master's head flew back, top hat quick to hit the ground, a low rumble of a moan spewing forth from between his full lips. He shot down the artist's throat, while I erupted onto the wall in front of me. Come dripped down George's chin and beard on one end of the wall and down plaster on the other.

After everyone cleaned up, George once again got down to business, and I did the same, my daily routine needing to get done. The only time I was called on was to serve the refreshments and eventually lunch and even dinner. As to the painting itself, it was covered up each time I entered the room. And, oh, how I ached to behold it, to see if George was as adept in his work as he was in all his other various talents.

But that, it seemed, would have to wait.

Days came and went, while George and I simply came and came. As to the master, he was, not too surprisingly, in glorious spirits all the while. And though I stopped spying on them after that first day, I was sure that as much coming was going on during the day as the night.

But still the painting remained hidden from prying eyes, the study locked up at night so that even I could not enter.

"How much longer do you have?" I asked my lover on his fifth night in my bed, my cock buried so far up his ass that it was a wonder it didn't jut out from his mouth.

"Tomorrow," he panted in reply. "Tomorrow it will be ready for its grand unveiling."

I stopped pumping his hole and stared into his mesmerizing eyes of blue. "And then you will...*leave?*"

He stroked my cheek as he slammed his ass into my cock. "It is what we *Bohemians* do, sweet James."

I nodded as I filled his rump with a veritable stream of come. "I shan't forget you, George."

He smiled as he shot his own stream, his aromatic, sticky load covering his chest in mere moments. "Of that I'm certain, James."

The next morning, before the rest of the staff and Byron Theodore and his wife were amassed to view the finished work, George snuck me into the study. The painting stood center-room on its easel, a sheet draped over it, the morning light turning the room to amber.

I was both excited and sad at what was to unfold: excited to see the work, sad that the artist would leave soon thereafter.

"Ready?" he asked.

I nodded. "Ready, sir."

He laughed. "You can't control that *sir* thing you do, can you, James?"

I shook my head from side to side. "It is like breathing for me, sir."

Though the breath was quickly knocked out of me when he grandly removed the sheet. The painting was large, the master taking center stage, looking as regal as any king ever had. The light, the shading, every crease in his suit and strand of hair hanging off his chin was perfect. "Genius," I managed, the word barely a reverent whisper.

"I had inspiration," he replied, patting my back, his hand coming to rest on my ass.

I smiled and then crouched down in front of the painting, my eyes squinting at the far left corner. "Is that...is that *you* in the reflection of the silver urn?"

His glorious chuckle filled my ears. "As I said, dear James, you will never forget me." And then he pointed to the far right corner, to the small lattice screen built into the wall. "And you shall be with me for generations to come."

Again I squinted, a tiny eye and nose visible behind the screen. "You knew?"

The chuckle grew, as did the swelling in my pants. "Of course, James. All manors have such rooms." Again he patted my back. "I told you he fancied me; I simply had to prove it."

I turned to him. "And up above the fireplace, no one will ever notice the hidden secrets this painting contains."

He shook his head and then kissed me on the cheek. "Just you and me, James."

We quickly hung the painting, to ensure that our secret would remain safe, and then I turned to him one final time, his kiss returned with one of my own. "Thank you...*George*." The kiss was repeated and repeated again. "For everything."

# ABOUT THE AUTHORS

**BRENT ARCHER** got serious about sharing his stories with the world in early 2012. His first story, "Dear Bryan," was published in the anthology *Virgin Ass*, and he has a second story coming out in a Cleis Press anthology later this year. When not writing, Brent enjoys singing, dancing, and gardening.

**XAVIER AXELSON** (xavieraxelson.com) sold his first short story in 2010 and hasn't stopped. As a writer-columnist, he has interviewed counterculture celebrities, artisans, singers, writers, performance artists, politicians and activists. In 2012, his first full-length work, *Velvet*, was released with Seventh Window Publications.

**MICHAEL BRACKEN** is the author of several books and almost one thousand short stories. His work has appeared in many previous Cleis Press anthologies, including *Best Gay Romance 2013* and *Best Gay Erotica 2013*. He lives and writes in Texas.

**DALE CHASE** has had 160 stories published over the past seventeen years. Her novel, *TAKEDOWN: Taming John Wesley Hardin*, was published in 2013, and *WYATT: Doc Holliday's Account of an Intimate Friendship* in 2012. Her collection *The Company He Keeps: Victorian Gentlemen's Erotica* won the Independent Publishers Association's IPPY silver medal.

**LANDON DIXON**'s writing credits include stories in the anthologies *Homo Thugs, Black Fire, Boy Fun, Who's Your Daddy?, The Sweeter the Juice, Big Holiday Packages, Best of Both, Brief Encounters, Hot Daddies, Hot Jocks, Uniforms Unzipped, Black Dungeon Masters, Indecent Exposures, Lust In Time* and *Best Gay Erotica 2009*.

**J. L. MERROW** is that rare beast: an English person who refuses to drink tea. She writes across genres, with a preference for contemporary gay romance, and is frequently accused of humor. Her novella, *Muscling Through*, was shortlisted for a 2013 EPIC e-book Award.

**SASHA PAYNE** is an English writer of gay erotic fiction and romance. She is a lifelong speculative fiction and fantasy fan and most enjoys working within the genres of speculative fiction, fantasy or historical fiction.

Among **FELICE PICANO**'s best-known works are *Like People in History, The Lure, Dryland's End, Twelve o'Clock Tales* and *The Joy of Gay Sex*. A second volume of his prize-winning nonfiction, *True Stories Too*, will be published in 2014. "Folly's Ditch" is from Picano's new, Victorian Era novel, *Ravenglass*.

**MICHAEL ROBERTS** was recently published in the MLR Press anthology *Lust in Time*, also edited by Rob Rosen. He is a frequent contributor to STARbooks Press, and his work has also appeared in a number of Alyson Books collections, on cruisingforsex.com and in several adult gay magazines, including *Mandate*.

**ALEX STITT** is a British-American raised in Cornwall whose observations of the gentry-class are primarily nostalgic. A Master of Psychology focusing on LGBT identity acquisition, he works as both a counselor and ally trainer throughout America while writing novels and short stories.

**SALOME WILDE** (salandtalerotica.com) writes erotica and queer romance in contemporary, historical, exotica and hard-boiled detective genres. Her stories appear in numerous anthologies and, with Talon Rihai, she is coauthor of the novella *After the First Taste of Love* (Storm Moon Press 2012) and the forthcoming *Turning Trick: A Boywhore's Tale*.

**LOGAN ZACHARY** (LoganZachary2002@yahoo.com) lives in Minneapolis, MN. *Calendar Boys* is a collection of his short stories. He has over a hundred erotic stories in print. His new erotic mystery, *Big Bad Wolf*, is a werewolf story set in Northern Minnesota.

# ABOUT
# THE EDITOR

ROB ROSEN (www.therobrosen.com), author of the novels *Sparkle: The Queerest Book You'll Ever Love*, *Divas Las Vegas*, *Hot Lava*, *Southern Fried*, *Queerwolf*, *Vamp*, and *Queens of the Apocalypse*, and editor of the anthology *Lust in Time*, has had short stories featured in more than two hundred anthologies.